THE CASTLE
IN THE
PYRENEES

Also by Jostein Gaarder:

Sophie's World

The Solitaire Mystery

The Christmas Mystery

Vita Brevis

Hello? Is Anybody There?

Through a Glass, Darkly

Maya

The Ringmaster's Daughter

The Orange Girl

THE
CASTLE
IN THE
PYRENEES

~

JOSTEIN GAARDER

Translated from the Norwegian by
JAMES ANDERSON

Weidenfeld & Nicolson
LONDON

First published in Great Britain in 2010
by Weidenfeld & Nicolson
An imprint of the Orion Publishing Group Ltd
Orion House, 5 Upper St Martin's Lane
London WC2H 9EA

An Hachette UK Company

First published in Norway as *Slottet i Pyreneene* in 2008
by Aschehoug & Co. (W. Nygaard), Oslo

This translation has been published
with the financial support of NORLA.

1 3 5 7 9 10 8 6 4 2

ISBN 978 0 297 85944 4 (cased)

All the characters in this book are fictitious, and any resemblance to
actual persons living or dead is purely coincidental.

A CIP catalogue record for this book is
available from the British Library.

Typeset by Input Data Services Ltd, Bridgwater, Somerset

Printed and bound in Great Britain by Clays Ltd, St Ives plc

The paper this book is printed on is certified by the ... that
are ... renewable and recyclable ...
made ... was grown ... ing
and ... to
the ... n.

I

☐ Well, Steinn, here I am. It was just magic to see you again. And out there too! You were so dumbfounded that you almost fell through the floor. That was no 'accidental meeting', you know. There were forces at work there, forces!

We had four hours to ourselves. Well, in a manner of speaking. Niels Petter wasn't too happy afterwards. He didn't say a word until we got to Førde.

We just strode up the valley. Half an hour later there we were by the birch copse once again ...

Neither of us said a word the whole time. About *that*, I mean. We talked about everything else, but not that. Just like in the old days. We hadn't managed to show a united front about what had happened. And so we withered on the vine, not you or me personally so much, but as a pair. We couldn't even say goodnight to each other. I remember spending that last night on the sofa. And I remember the smell of your cigarette smoke from the other room. I felt I could see your bowed neck through the wall and the closed door. You were just sitting hunched at the desk smoking. I moved out the next day, and we'd not seen each other since, not for more than thirty years. It's unbelievable.

Then suddenly, after all those years, we're awoken like Sleeping Beauties – as if by the same miraculous alarm clock! And we travel all the way out there quite independently. On the same day, Steinn, in a new century, in a totally new world. Suddenly it's 'Hi!' after more than thirty years.

Don't tell me that was just chance. Don't tell me there are no forces guiding us!

The most surrealistic thing of all was when the lady who owns the hotel suddenly came out on to the balcony – she was the young daughter of the house back then. More than thirty years had passed for her too. I think it must have been *the* déjà vu of her life. Do you remember what she said? 'So nice to see that you're still together,' were her words. They hurt. But they were also quite droll too, considering that you and I hadn't seen each other since we looked after her three small girls one morning in the middle of the 1970s. We did it as a thank you for the loan of the bicycles and the transistor radio.

They're calling me now. It's a July evening, don't forget, and here by the sea the summer holidays are in full swing.

I think they're grilling some trout on the barbecue, and here comes Niels Petter with a drink for me. He's given me ten minutes to finish off, and I need them, because there's something important I want to ask you.

Can we make a solemn promise to delete every email we send each other after we've read them? I mean straight away, right then and there, and that naturally means no printouts either.

I see this new contact as a stream of thought vibrating between two souls rather than an exchange of corre- spondence which will be there between us forever. But a bonus would be that we could allow ourselves to write about everything.

We've both got spouses, and we've got children. I don't like the thought of having our messages just sitting there inside the machine.

We don't know when we're going to make our exits. But one day we'll pass away from this carnival with all its masks and roles, and only a few transient props will remain after us, until they too are swept away.

We will step outside time, leave what we call 'reality'.

The years pass, but I can't escape the feeling that some- thing connected with what happened all those years ago may suddenly pop up again. Occasionally I sense that something is hard on my heels, breathing down my neck.

I can't forget the flashing blue lights at Leikanger, and

I still start each time a police car is behind me. Once, some years ago, a policeman came to the door. He must have seen how jumpy I was. But he only wanted to find an address in the neighbourhood.

I'm sure you think I'm worrying myself unnecessarily. Any criminal offence must be obsolete by now anyway.

But shame doesn't become obsolete ...

So promise me that you'll delete them!

It wasn't until we were sitting amongst the ruins of the old shepherd's hut that you told me why you'd come. You tried to explain what you'd been doing over the past thirty years, and you described your climate project. Then you managed to say a little bit about a particularly intense dream you'd had the night before we met each other on the balcony. It was a cosmic dream, you said, but you weren't able to get much further because those heifers came frisking towards us and actually chased us down the valley again. After that, nothing more was said about the dream.

But your cosmic dreams are only to be expected ... We had tried to sleep for a few hours, but we were too excited, naturally we were, and so instead we lay there with our eyes closed, whispering together. About stars and galaxies and things like that. Just about big, distant, higher things ...

It's strange to think about now. That was before I *believed* in anything. But only just before.

They're calling me again. Just one final comment before I send this. That lake was called Eldrevatnet. Isn't that an odd name for a mountain lake so far from civilisation? I mean, who were these 'eldre', these ancient folk, up there amongst the rocks and peaks?

When I drove by it recently with Niels Petter, I just stared at the road atlas. I hadn't been back since, and I couldn't look up, not at the lake. Some minutes later we rounded the next spot as well, I mean the bend by the precipice, and that was the most painful place to pass.

I don't think I looked up from the atlas until we were down in the valley. And so I learnt lots of place names, and I read them out to Niels Petter. I had to occupy myself with something. I was afraid I'd go to pieces and be forced to tell him everything.

Then we arrived at the new tunnels. I insisted that we drive through them, rather than past the stave-church and down on to the old road by the river. I made some excuse about it being late and we were short of time.

Ah, Lake Eldrevatnet.

The Lingonberry Woman was 'old'. At least we thought so then. An elderly woman, we said. An elderly woman with a pink shawl across her shoulders. We had to make sure that what we'd seen was the same thing at least. That was when we were still on speaking terms.

5

The truth is that she was the same age as I am today, no more and no less. She was what we might call a middle-aged woman.

When you came out on to the balcony, it was like coming face to face with myself. It had been thirty years since we'd seen each other. But it wasn't only that. I felt so clearly that I could see myself from the outside, I mean from your point of view and with your eyes. All of a sudden it was as if I was the Lingonberry Woman. That was the unsettling feeling that came over me.

They're calling me again. It's the third time, so now I'll just send and delete. Warm wishes from Solrun.

I can hardly stop myself putting 'your Solrun', because there was never any breach between us. I just took a few of my things that day and left. But I didn't return. It was almost a year before I wrote from Bergen asking you to pack up and send the rest of my stuff, and even then I didn't regard it as a formal parting of any sort, it was simply the most practical arrangement, as I'd been so long on the other side of the country. It was several years before I met Niels Petter. And it took you more than a decade to find Berit.

You were patient. You never really gave up on us. I've sometimes suffered from the feeling of living like a bigamist.

———

6

I'll never forget what took place on that mountain road. Sometimes it feels as if hardly an hour passes without me thinking about it.

But then something happened afterwards, and that really *was* a marvellous and uplifting event. Now I see it as a gift.

If only we'd been able to accept that gift together! But we were terrified. At first you just collapsed and let me comfort you. Then you suddenly took off.

After a few days we'd already begun to drift apart. We'd lost the ability or the will to look into each other's eyes.

Us two, Steinn. It was unbelievable.

☐ Solrun, Solrun! How beautiful you were! So resplendent in your red dress with your back to the fjord and the white railings!

I recognised you straight away, of course I did. Or was I seeing things? But it was you – as if you were the product of a completely different epoch.

And let me say right away: I certainly did not associate you with any 'Lingonberry Woman'.

To think that you've written! I've been hoping all these weeks that you really would. The idea of using email was mine, but it was you who said, just before parting, that you'd make contact when it was convenient, and so the first move was yours.

It *is* staggering to think of us chancing to meet again in the same backwater as before. It was as if we'd been living with a long-standing tryst to come together just then and there. But there was no agreement. It was an extraordinary fluke.

I came walking out of the dining room carrying a cup and saucer, and in my confusion some of the coffee spilt and I scalded my wrist, and how right you are in saying I only just managed to keep my feet – I had to stop the cup crashing to the floor.

I exchanged a brief greeting with your husband, who suddenly busied himself fetching something from the car, you and I managed to have a few words, and then the hotel proprietress came out. Perhaps she'd seen me pass reception and actually remembered me from all those years before when the hotel had been her mother's.

You and I were now standing tête-à-tête, and she obviously took us for a middle-aged husband and wife who, aeons before, had come out for a romantic trip to this arm of the fjord before settling down and spending the rest of their lives together – I've tried to imagine it – before eventually, perhaps in an acute attack of nostalgia, returning to the scenes of their youthful escapade. So, of course, we'd have to go out on to the balcony after breakfast, and although we'd given up smoking – politically correct as we both were – that was reasonable enough. We'd have to go out and see the copper beeches, the fjord and the mountains. We'd always done that back then.

The hotel had a different reception, and there was a new café for passing trade. But the trees, the fjord and the mountains were the same. So was the furniture and the paintings in the lounge too; even the billiard table stood there just as it used to, and I doubt if the old piano has been tuned. You played Debussy on it, and you played nocturnes by Chopin. I'll never forget how the other guests gathered round the piano and applauded you heartily.

Thirty years had passed, yet time had stood almost still.

I've managed to overlook the only real alteration. The tunnels were new! We had arrived by boat and we'd left by boat. There was no alternative in those days.

Remember how it soothed our fears when the last ferry had arrived? After that the village was cut off and we had all the rest of the evening, the night and the next morning until the *Nesøy* nosed out of the fjord and returned with more passengers before lunch. Hours of grace, we called them. Now presumably we'd have had to sit on the veranda all evening checking every car that emerged from the tunnel. Would they all carry on westwards, or would one of them turn off at the Glacier Museum and come to the hotel to fetch us – I mean to take us into custody?

———

By the way, I'd forgotten that we'd looked after her daughters. So, you see, I don't remember everything.

I agree to your idea about deleting the emails as soon as we've read them, then to delete the reply as soon as it's been sent. I don't like having too much lying about on disk either. Sometimes it can be liberating just to give one's ideas and associations an airing. Nowadays far too many words are stored and archived on the Internet, and on memory sticks and hard disks.

So I deleted the email you sent me a good while ago and have sat down to reply. And I must confess that this business of deleting has its drawbacks as well, because as I sit here I already long for the opportunity to reread one of the passages you wrote. Now I'll have to do it from memory, and that's how this exchange of emails will have to proceed.

You intimate that there could have been some supernatural forces at work behind our remarkable reunion out there on the hotel veranda, and I'll have to ask for your forbearance right from the start when it comes to such questions, because I'll be expressing myself as candidly as I did in the past. I can only regard such chance meetings as fortuitous occurrences that are neither willed nor controlled in any way. It's true that in this case it was a *huge* coincidence and not just something insignificant. But you

must also take into account all the days we don't experience things of that kind.

At the risk of fanning the flames of your penchant for the
occult, I will admit something to you. When I travelled by
bus and came out of the long tunnel up by Bergshovden,
the fjord was shrouded in mist and I couldn't see anything
below me. The summits were visible, but the fjord and the
valleys had been erased from the landscape. Then came
another tunnel, and when we emerged from that, I was
beneath the cloud cover. I saw the fjord and the three
valley bottoms, but now I couldn't see the mountainsides
any more.

I was thinking, But is she here? Is she coming too?

Then you arrived. The next morning you were standing
on the veranda in an almost girlish summer dress when
I came out of the dining room balancing a brimful cup of
coffee.

It felt as if I was the one who'd put you there, as if it was
I who'd written you into the old hotel on just that day. It
was as if you'd been born on the veranda out of my memory
and my loss.

But it's hardly surprising that I had you very much in my
thoughts, now that I suddenly found myself back in the
place we'd once nicknamed our 'erotic backwater'.
Although arriving at the same time was of course pure,
complete luck.

———

I'd been sitting at breakfast thinking of you while I drank my orange juice and cracked open an egg. I was totally immersed in the vivid dream I'd had. Then I took my coffee out on to the veranda. And, hey presto – there you were!

I felt sorry for your husband. He had my full sympathy when, an hour later, we left him and headed into the mountains in our *own* twosome.

The way we walked, and the way we began to talk, seemed a delightful echo of the time we were here in the first flush of youth. The valley was the same, and as I said, You still look young.

But I don't believe in destiny, Solrun. I really don't.

You mention the 'Lingonberry Woman' again. And that touches on one of the strangest things I've ever experienced. I haven't forgotten her, you see, and I'm not denying her existence either. But wait a moment. There was something I witnessed on my way home.

When both of you had left, I stayed on for the opening of the new Climate Centre next morning. As I told you, I was to make a small speech about it at lunch. So it was on Friday morning that I took the express boat from Balestrand to Flåm, and after a few hours' wait there, got the train to Myrdal and then a connection to Oslo.

Just before we got up to Myrdal, the train from Flåm stopped at a great waterfall called Kjosfossen. The tourists were practically herded out of the train to photograph the waterfall, or at least look up at the chalk-white cascade.

As we stood there on the platform, a *nymph* suddenly appeared on the slope to the right of the waterfall. It was as if she appeared out of nothing. Just as suddenly she disappeared again, but only for a split second, because she reappeared forty or fifty metres away. This was repeated a couple of times more.

Well, what do you think of that? Perhaps if you're a sprite you don't have to obey natural laws.

But let's not be too quick to jump to conclusions. Had I seen a vision or a ghost? A couple of hundred other people had also experienced exactly the same thing as me. So had we all been witnesses to something supernatural, then, I mean to a real naiad or natural spirit? No, no. The whole thing was obviously arranged for tourists, and the only thing I can't work out is how much pay the girls were on.

But is there anything I've forgotten? Yes – despite all this, the girl didn't move across the landscape in a natural manner, she leapt from place to place at lightning speed. There was that too. But it was a trick! Just how many 'sprites' there were by Kjosfossen that afternoon, I have no idea. I assume that there were only two or three, and they were all paid the same.

I'm telling you this because I've realised something that perhaps we never thought about at the time, but which I don't think it's too late to consider. The 'Lingonberry

Woman' could have been planted somehow. She might have been playing a part, playing a trick on us, and it's possible we weren't the only victims of her bogus lingonberry whims. Eccentric rustics like her exist almost everywhere.

But again, is there something I've forgotten? There certainly is! It wasn't just that she seemed to come from nothing and nowhere, but as soon as she'd performed her sketch, the earth simply swallowed her up. And perhaps it literally did. Perhaps she was a practical joker who simply sank into some old pitfall or behind some detritus, how can I tell? We didn't examine the ground; the truth is that we ran full pelt up the valley as if the devil himself were on our heels.

Sometimes we say, I won't believe it until I see it. But I'm not sure we even need to believe it then. We ought at least to rub our eyes on occasions before we judge. We need to ask ourselves how something or someone has managed to trick us so completely. We didn't do that back then. We were terrified. And we'd been destabilised by what had happened a few days earlier. If one of us had flipped, the other would certainly have done so too.

Please don't feel yourself rebuffed. I was so happy to see you again, and now I go round smiling most of the time. I'm not saying that such lucky coincidences are unimportant or meaningless. They can be highly significant because they grab our attention and influence us. They can also be very important for what happens subsequently.

Of all places it was *there* we were to be reunited. So we just walked up to the shepherd's hut once more. Who would have thought such a thing could happen again?

A hike of four hours isn't a long time if you still have the occasional meeting, say once or twice a year. But when several decades have elapsed since your last encounter, four hours is a very long time. For then the difference between that one meeting and nothing at all is enormous.

☐ OK, Steinn. It's nice to hear from you, but it's also a reminder of why we drifted apart. One reason was that, then as now, we had very different interpretations of certain things we experienced together. Another was that you always spoke so patronisingly about my explanation.

But it *is* nice to hear from you. I miss you. Just give me a little time, and I'll reply when I'm in a better mood.

☐ I didn't mean to be patronising, but I can't remember my exact words any more. What did I say? Didn't I say that I go round the house chuckling because we've seen each other again?

Anyway, I have more to tell. I travelled out on a ferry with the same name as the arm of the fjord. The first place we put in to was Hella, where we'd once parked that awful old car of ours – it was so strange to stand on deck looking down on the ferry quay – but then we crossed the main fjord to Vangsnes before we turned about and arrived at Balestrand. There, I paced up and down the point by the Kvikne Hotel waiting for the express boat from Bergen. It arrived a little late, I think it was half an hour behind time, and as I was going aboard, I discovered that the name of the boat was the *Solundir*!

I started. I thought of you of course. I hadn't thought of much else since we'd waved goodbye from the old steamship quay a couple of days previously. But now I began to remember that summer we were out on the Solund islands, when we visited your grandmother. Wasn't she called Randi? Randi Hjønnevåg?

I didn't merely fall into a reverie, I would describe it more as a particular state of consciousness, for suddenly a whole cascade of old experiences flashed through my mind, vivid images and impressions from the time we were out by the sea when we were just twenty-something, almost like film clips from episodes I couldn't remember filming, and they weren't silent films either, because I seemed to be able to hear your voice, I could hear you laughing and talking to me. Didn't I also hear the breeze and the seabirds, and couldn't I smell your long, dark hair? It smelt of sea and kelp. This was no ordinary kind of thought process, it came welling up like a geyser of suppressed bliss, like a flashback to a time which once had been ours.

First, I meet you up there at the old hotel more than thirty years after we were there last, and when I leave, it's on a boat named after the tiny island group where your mother's family came from. Didn't you use to say that your own name is almost an echo of that one? We two usually talked about Ytre Sula, which was the name of the outermost island where your grandmother lived. But Solrun and Solundir! Was it strange I started?

But we mustn't be tempted to draw any occult con-clusions from such chance webs of connections. The boat was quite simply named after one of the county's admin-istrative centres, no more than that. So I calmed down. But I stood on the deck for a long time, smiling.

Well, what do you think?

☐ I'm out there now. In Solund, I mean. I'm in the old house at Kolgrov sitting looking out across reefs and islands. The only thing ruining the view at the moment is a pair of man's legs. Niels Petter is standing on a ladder painting the upstairs window frames.

When you and I came down from the shepherd's hut that Wednesday, my husband thought it important to leave as soon as possible, because he said we ought at least to try to get home to Bergen in time for the six o'clock news.

It was already around three when we drove up Bøyadal and into the tunnel near the glacier. When we emerged again, we noticed how the mist was lifting and the sun was coming through as we drove along Lake Jølstravatnet. And the mist was the only subject Niels Petter commented on until we'd passed Førde. It's lifting, he said. That was as we rounded the lake near Skei. I tried to start a conversation, but I couldn't get any more out of him. Later it occurred to me that this laconic comment may have been more than just meteorological, that it may have been as much about his own mood as the mist.

As we drove southwards from Førde, he turned to me and said that it was a long journey all in one day, and that we might spend a night out at the house that had belonged to my mother's family, which we now call our 'summer cabin'. The original idea had been to travel straight home, mainly because of his plans for the following day, but the suggestion he was making now was his attempt at reconciliation, both for being so grumpy when I insisted on taking a long walk with you – after all those years, Steinn – and then for sitting silent in the car for so long afterwards. So we did. We crossed the fjord between Rysjedalsvika and Rutledal, and carried on to the Solund islands. We had a marvellous day out there by the sea while you were attending the opening of the Climate Centre. Naturally enough I sent various thoughts to you,

I mean memories and images, times we'd shared, and that was something I went on doing over the next few days. They were intense memories and some of them obviously reached you as the little 'film clips' you couldn't remember filming . . .

We arrived home in Bergen late on Thursday evening, and early on Friday morning I went down to Strandkaien to watch the *Solundir* slip her moorings. She departs from Bergen at eight o'clock. You'd said you'd be leaving Balestrand that morning, and as I'd got up early anyway I took a morning stroll down from Skansen across the Fish Market to the docks. To wish you bon voyage, Steinn, to say goodbye once more. Call me irrational, but I just felt I wanted to. Don't try telling me that my greeting didn't reach you. It was nice to think you'd be travelling on the *Solundir*, and I imagined that you'd probably start reminiscing about me and our summer escapade out here.

No, the boat isn't named after me. As you mention it takes its name from the islands at the mouth of Sognefjord, where I'd been almost the whole of the previous day, and where I'm sitting at the moment looking across the sea as I write. Fortunately, the legs have gone now; they were somewhat distracting both for the view and my thoughts . . .

Solundir is simply a Norse plural of *Solund*, and there are many hundreds of islands in the Solund group. *Sól* means 'furrow' and *–und* means 'filled with'. The Solund islands are filled with furrows. That's no loose description of the geology here. 'Furrowed, weathered o'er the sea . . .' as our national anthem says.

I'm sure you remember how we used to chase about playing hide-and-seek amongst the psychedelic rock formations, which are made up of a brightly coloured conglomerate, and you can't have forgotten how we walked for hours collecting stones in that sculptured land-scape. You collected marble, and I collected a particular type of red stone. They're still here, glowing, both yours and mine. I use them round the flower beds.

You're right that my grandmother's name was Randi, and I must admit to a certain disappointment that you even need to ask, because the two of you got on so well together. I remember that you once described Grandma as the warmest and loveliest person you'd ever met. She was forever going out into her little garden humming, Oh, how nice that Steinn is! to herself. There was something quite special about 'that Steinn'. Grandma had never met such a wonderful young man.

My mother grew up out here too, as you know, on what is now the most westerly inhabited place in the country. Her maiden name was Hjønnevåg, you remembered that too, and when they gave me the name Solrun my parents didn't just pluck the name out of thin air, it was partly inspired by the family background.

---

*

Now we're all out here again, all four of us in fact, before school and our routine lives take over in a few days' time. Ingrid is now a student! The air out here in the mouth of the fjord is unusually still, and yesterday we could sit out in the garden and have a barbecue for once.

The world isn't a mosaic of coincidences, Steinn. It's all interconnected.

☐ It's great that you've replied. So I see that fortunately it didn't take long for your humour to improve.

Just think that you're *there* now. So I suppose I'm a little bit there myself too, as we're corresponding. I'm the first to admit that two people can be in close proximity even though the physical distance between them is great. In that sense I agree that the world is interconnected.

I'm so moved that you went down to Strandkaien that morning to send a greeting to me via the express boat. I can see you in my mind's eye running down all the steps from Skansen, and the sight puts me in mind of a Spanish film. I can now at least acknowledge that your greeting has arrived, even if I couldn't before.

☐ But at one point, when we were going up Mundalsdal, you said that you rejected all 'so-called supernatural

phenomena'. You proclaimed your non-belief in telepathy, or any form of second sight or clairvoyance. You
made that assertion even after I'd given you some excellent examples of them. In your case it's probably a matter
of not using the antennae you've got, of keeping the
blinkers on, or perhaps not recognising that you sometimes 'receive' things you think are your own inspiration.

But you're not alone, Steinn. There's a lot of psychic
blindness in our age, and a lot of spiritual poverty.

I am naive enough not to be able to brush aside, as
a simple coincidence, the fact that we happened to be
standing together on that hotel veranda again. I believe
these things are controlled in some way. Don't ask me
how or why, because I really don't know. But not knowing
isn't the same thing as shutting one's eyes. King Oedipus
didn't see the threads of destiny that were manipulating
him, and when it did become clear to him, he felt so
disgraced that he blinded himself. But he'd been blind to
his destiny all along, of course.

☐ This has become a bit like ping-pong, so perhaps we
should carry on emailing throughout the afternoon? I'll
then be able to enjoy Solund a bit myself this summer's
day. Eh?

☐ Why not, we're having a conversation. I'm on holiday,
and in this house we have an unwritten rule that on days

22

off everyone does what they want. We're only strict about eating together. Apart from breakfast, that is; we help ourselves to that as we get up. But it's not long since lunch, and now I have no commitments until we have dinner late this evening. If the wind doesn't rise, it might be barbecue weather again today.

And you? I mean, what will *I* be visiting this afternoon?

☐ Sadly, I can offer nothing to match your surroundings. I'm sitting in a boring office at the University of Oslo, and I'll be here until I meet Berit in town around seven o'clock. We're going to Bærum to visit her elderly but mentally alert and very witty father. But that's a long way off, and so we've got several hours together.

☐ Don't forget that I studied at Oslo University for five years. Those years, Steinn ... For me it's sufficiently exotic just dreaming of those years.

But back then I don't think you ever had any expectations of becoming a professor at the University. Wasn't your ambition to teach at a secondary school?

☐ But I found I had an almost frightening amount of time to fill after you'd left, and that initially turned into a doctorate and then a research fellowship. But perhaps we should wait a bit before talking about 'then'. I'm interested in who you are now.

––––––

23

☐ Well, I was the one who became the secondary school teacher. We spoke about that, and honestly I've never regretted it. I regard it as a privilege to earn my living by spending a few hours each day with committed young people, and what's more teaching subjects that interest me. It's not a mere cliché that you keep learning all the time you have pupils. In most classes I've taught there's been some blond curlyhead who's awakened memories of you and of us in the old days, and one year there was a boy who really was like you, he almost had your voice too.

But the floor is yours. I wrote something along the lines of not regarding it as a coincidence that we suddenly found ourselves standing on that balcony again.

☐ Yes, that was it. The very words 'chance meeting' or 'fluke' point by definition towards something which, statistically speaking, is unlikely. I once calculated that the chances of throwing twelve sixes with a dice, I mean twelve sixes one after another, is less than one in two billion. That doesn't mean that someone hasn't thrown the same number with a dice twelve times in a row, for the simple reason that there are several billion people on the planet, and dice are thrown almost everywhere. But in an exceptional case like that, we're talking about odds of astronomical dimensions, and when it does happen, people sometimes begin to laugh hysterically, because in statistical terms you'd have to sit throwing dice for thousands of years to have a reasonable chance of getting a series of twelve the same, though of course it could happen quite spontaneously, just in the course of a few seconds. Isn't that a lovely thought?

It was certainly an amazing coincidence to bump into you there. It was a shock. I wouldn't hesitate to call it a stroke of luck either. But 'supernatural' it wasn't.

☐ Are you quite certain of that?

☐ Almost completely certain, yes. Just as I also feel certain that there is no fate, guiding hand or mental power that is capable of influencing the outcome of, for example, a game of dice. There can be cheating and sleight of hand, to be sure, there can be lapses of memory and misreporting, but physical events *literally* cannot be influenced either by fate, divine providence or by the pseudo-phenomenon which some people call psychokinesis.

Have you ever heard of anyone making a fortune at roulette because he or she was able by the power of thought to control or foresee precisely where the ball would end up on the wheel? A few seconds of clairvoyance would be enough to make you a millionaire. But no one has such gifts. No one! That's why there are no notices outside casinos saying that mind-readers and psychics are not admitted. Such prohibitions aren't necessary.

———

*

We must also consider another dimension, both of games of chance and of our lives more generally. The world's most amazing flukes have an innate tendency to be remembered and carefully preserved by the culture we live in, and by the untrained observer a whole raft of anecdotes about extraordinary events may easily be mistaken for 'forces' which exist almost everywhere and affect our lives.

In my opinion it's crucial to understand this mechanism. Even the selection of Lottery winners that is remembered and passed on is reminiscent of Darwin's theory of natural selection. The only difference is that in our case we're talking about an *artificial* selection. Unfortunately, this can easily create artificial notions.

More or less consciously, we may begin to correlate circumstances that are unrelated. This, I believe, is a typically human characteristic. Unlike animals, we often seek an underlying cause, for example a destiny, a providence or some other controlling principle, even where there is none.

So I think meeting each other out there that day was complete coincidence. The chances of it happening were minimal – neither of us had been there since – but even if the chance was minimal, that in itself is no indication that it was anything other than a huge fluke.

If we managed to gather together the full panoply of history's most striking examples of significant coincidences into one fat volume – i.e. all the winning tickets – we'd have to make space for several trillion other volumes if we wished to include all the losing tickets as well. But there aren't enough trees to make all these books. There isn't even enough room on our planet for so many trees or books.

But just for a change I'll focus on one single losing ticket, and ask, Can you ever remember reading a decent-sized interview with anyone who *hadn't* won the Lottery?

☐ You haven't changed much. And that's good too, Steinn. There's something boyish and fresh about your stubbornness.

But perhaps you're blind. Perhaps you're both narrow-minded and short-sighted.

Do you remember that Magritte picture of a huge lump of rock floating above the ground? I think it had a small castle on top. You can't have forgotten that picture.

But if you'd witnessed something similar today, you would certainly have tried to explain it away. Maybe you'd have said it was a trick. That the rock was hollow and filled with helium. Or that it was supported by an ingenious network of invisible pulleys and wires.

I'm a much simpler soul. I would probably just have raised my arms to the boulder and sung out my 'hallelujah' or my 'amen'.

*

In your first mail you wrote, 'Sometimes we say, I won't believe it until I see it. But I'm not sure we even need to believe it then ...'

I must say this statement troubles me a little. To my ears it does sound rather unempirical not to trust the evidence of one's senses. To tell you the truth, it sounds a bit medieval ...

If the senses conveyed something that didn't accord with Aristotle, it was the senses that were wrong, and when observations of planets' orbits didn't fit in with the geocentric view of the world, they invented some humbug called epicycles to explain what the eye saw. The men of the Church and Inquisition also practised the self-censorship of refusing to look through Galileo's telescope. But you know all that.

Have you considered that we two actually *did* witness something like a great mass of rock floating above the moss and heather. A miracle. A miracle beyond this world! And, let me add, we saw exactly the same thing, we were in complete agreement about that.

☐ Were we?

☐ Yes, quite definitely. But to get back to our reunion out there, couldn't we make an attempt to lay all these threads of destiny aside?

28

☐ What do you mean?

☐ Perhaps this 'coincidence' was something as banal as a bit of telepathy. But maybe that makes little difference to you if you've already made up your mind that you don't 'believe' in thought transference either.

You believe in gravity. But can you explain it?

Maybe you ought to give me a chance and at least take a peep into my Galileo telescope?

☐ I can't explain gravity. It simply exists. And yes of course I'll look into your Galileo telescope. If you had a dozen telescopes, I'd look into them all. Well, hand me the first.

☐ As far as Niels Petter and I were concerned it was a very spontaneous trip, and I'm certain I was the one who suggested we should spend a day at Fjærland visiting the Book Town and the Glacier Museum. We were really on our way back from the east of the country to Bergen, but I thought that after all those years we ought to be able to make a little detour up there, even though it would certainly cause me some pain. The idea popped up as a sudden inspiration. It really was something that just came to me.

You had a much longer planning horizon, so in this case it must have been you who were the transmitter and me the receiver. It wouldn't have been that odd if you'd transmitted the thought that, for the first time since the two of us stayed in the old hotel, you were going there again. The point is simply that you have no idea when you're transmitting or receiving. You don't feel anything in your head when you're thinking, either. Even if you're thinking of something very dramatic, violent or sad, you don't *feel* a crunching, splintering or squeaking inside your head. That's because thoughts don't usually have anything to do with the body or physical processes.

To me the simplest explanation for how we happened to turn up simultaneously at the place that had once been both the loveliest and the bitterest spot in our lives is telepathy. Your explanation or explaining away is more complicated and to me smacks of dull statistics.

In terms of pure probabilities, our reunion on the old balcony was roughly the same as if we'd stood on opposite sides of the fjord and each fired a rifle bullet, and these had collided in mid-fjord and sunk to the bottom as one body. That *might* have been supernatural. It would have to be called miraculous precision at all events. And so I find it much easier to conceive of two souls which had once been intimate being able to communicate with each other over a distance about something they both find deeply emotional. You sent me a signal that you were going out there again, and I received your signal. And then I arrived!

———

Telepathy, in fact. This well-documented phenomenon I'm now introducing as a reasonable explanation for what you brush aside as an 'extraordinary fluke' has been the subject of experimental research by many people at various universities across the world; amongst the pioneers were the husband-and-wife team the Rhines at Duke University, North Carolina way back in the 1930s. If you want, I can easily send you some references, I've got a whole bibliography.

Isn't it also true that quantum mechanics has shown us how everything in the universe is interconnected, down to the minutest particle?

With the aid of certain colleagues I've actually read up a bit on quantum mechanics recently. At my school we've had an interdisciplinary seminar in the evenings for the past year. The club itself is simply called In vino veritas, and perhaps that says something about its laid-back style, but having spent some evenings with physicists and natural scientists, I don't get the feeling that modern physics has made the world any less mysterious than it was in Plato's time. But correct me, Steinn, if you think that's wrong.

If two particles, for example two photons, have a common origin or starting point and then are split and travel away from each other at high speed, both particles will still just as much remain part of the same whole. Even if they are sent out into space in different directions and light years separate them, they will remain interlinked: each of the particles will have information about the characteristics of the other. This is obviously nothing to do with communication, but with *interdependence*, or what is called non-locality. On the quantum level the world actually is non-local. It's strange – perhaps as incomprehensible as gravity – and Einstein refuted the phenomenon because he saw it as inimical to reason, but post-Einstein it has been verified experimentally.

Now we're not talking about telepathy, but about tele-physics. Although in my opinion spiritual contact over large distances is more relevant to mankind than quantum mechanics – simply because we are the spirits here. Glance up at the stars and galaxies. Look up at passing comets and asteroids and have a good laugh. Huge heavenly bodies they may be, but *we* are the living souls in this universe. What do comets or asteroids know? What are they capable of perceiving about anything? What self-consciousness do they possess?

If I were superstitious I would have said that photons have consciousness and that they telecommunicate by sending thoughts to each other. Well, I don't believe that. I believe that we human beings are in a unique position. We are spirits in this theatre of the universe!

Steinn! While you're reading this sentence billions of

---

neutrinos are streaming through your brain. They come from the sun, they come from other stars in the Milky Way, and they come from other galaxies in the universe. They are also, in their way, an expression of the non-locality of the universe.

Another paradox is that particles in quantum mechanics sometimes behave in wave form and sometimes like particles. Experiments have shown that an electron, which is a small particle of matter or 'thing', is capable of going through two different openings or holes at once. This is about as amazing as imagining a single tennis ball simultaneously going through two different holes in the fence round a tennis court.

I don't ask you to explain or go into details about how something can be both a wave and a particle, or sometimes one or the other. I ask you for nothing more than to acknowledge the universe as it actually is. If the laws of physics are mysterious – in our eyes, I mean – they'll just have to be. It's possible to rue the fact that we can't explain everything under the sun – poets could turn this into a reasonable daily exercise – by which I mean an elegiac shake of the head directed at how little we comprehend of the deeply mysterious universe we find ourselves in – but for the moment we must just accept it.

That you can send me a thought which I, more or less consciously, am capable of picking up maybe isn't comprehensible from what we can currently construe

---

mathematically or physically. But perhaps it's no more difficult to acknowledge than mainstream quantum physics?

What do you think?

The British mathematician and astrophysicist James Jeans once said that the universe was beginning to look more like a great thought than a great machine

☐ I've just received the very latest climate report, which is more alarming than we feared, and a couple of excited journalists have been in touch. They absolutely must have a comment before their deadline. There's a certain amount of media-induced hysteria about such questions these days. So I'll have to break off from our conversation for a while, but it won't take all afternoon. Until then, let me say that I respect your conviction, and more than that: no matter what 'isms' divide us today, I rate you very highly as a person. So you'll have to forgive me for not believing in so-called extrasensory phenomena myself.

☐ That's fine. There are many layers to you, young man. I knew you once, so now I'm going to write a few words about the Lingonberry Woman. On that occasion you cried afterwards, you sobbed like child, and I had to rock you.

And what happened more than thirty years later when we were up there again? I can sense how you're fighting against it, the way I felt I could see you through that wall and door the night you sat in the bedroom and smoked, but now you must listen to me.

You wrote that you don't believe in any unknown forces affecting our lives. But up there you trembled like an aspen leaf when we stood in front of that birch copse again. And the body doesn't lie.

As we got closer you suddenly grasped my hand. Long ago we often walked hand in hand, but it was extraordinary to grab my hand just then. Even though I realised that it must be because we were getting near and you needed support. Because you were frightened! At all events you were hardly the stalwart male up there by the birch slope. You feared something beyond this world.

You've got a strong hand, Steinn. But it trembled!

I was also affected by the intensity of the moment. But I was calmer than you, I was more at one with myself, and perhaps that was because I'd already arrived at a kind of conviction regarding the afterlife. The paranormal is normal to me. I was prepared for the possibility that she'd materialise again. Although the term materialise is completely misleading, as she wasn't physical. It might not even have been possible to capture her on film. She was what we call an *apparition*. Both history and parapsychology are full of reports of such phenomena, stories about one person who has appeared to the soul of another, even though the pair may have been hundreds of miles apart in the physical world. The literature is also replete with accounts of those who have seen and received messages from people who have recently – not died, but *risen again*. The best-known example, of course, is Jesus. But we live in a highly materialistic culture which has almost no contact at all with the spiritual – not to mention the hereafter. But look at Shakespeare, read the Icelandic sagas, take another glance at the Bible and Homer. Or listen to what other cultures have to say about their shamans and ancestors.

But, you know, I believe that her appearance at that time might have been to *comfort* us more than anything. Because there was something about what you call her 'sketch' that I've thought about countless times since. She didn't look at us with an accusing or hateful expression. She regarded us with mildness. She smiled. She'd already gone over to the other side, where there is no hate. If there isn't any matter, there is obviously no hate either.

However, at the time it was a very upsetting experience for both of us – for me too. We were petrified. But then we'd been petrified for a week already. If she'd appeared again, I would have received her with open arms.

But this time she didn't show up . . .

There is no death, Steinn. And there are no dead.

———

II

☐ I'm back now. Are you still at your PC?

☐ I'm pacing round it, Steinn. What did the new climate report say?

☐ It was fairly alarming, and it indicates that the bulletins from the UN's Intergovernmental Panel on Climate Change have been far too conservative up to now. They've placed too little weight on so-called feedback mechanisms. Put succinctly, this means that the hotter it gets, the hotter it goes on getting. When the snow and ice of the Arctic melt, less sunlight is reflected, and the earth as a whole becomes more heated. This in turn leads to the permafrost melting and releasing more greenhouse gases, like methane. And there are several such self-reinforcing mechanisms. Perhaps we're approaching the fatal tipping point, and after that there'll be no return from a global catastrophe. It isn't long since most of us thought it would take half a century for all the sea ice to vanish from the Arctic in the summer months. Now we see the process taking place much faster than expected; we're only talking about a couple of decades perhaps. The disappearance of the ice in the north also helps to hasten the melting of glaciers in Asia, Africa and South America, with the result that these vital water reservoirs are reduced and watercourses are dry for part of the year, something that obviously affects crop yields and the supply of drinking water to millions of people. But it's not just human beings that are vulnerable. The report points out that as much as 50 per cent of the earth's plant and animal species are threatened.

What are we doing to our planet? That's the question. We have only one, and we must share it with the people who come after us.

But we're having a conversation. Do you want me to go on?

☐ Yes, do go on. I'm going into the living room to tidy through some papers and periodicals, but I'll run back in as soon as I hear my machine ping.

☐ Naturally that picture by Magritte is vivid in my memory. It was the eye-catching poster we put up in our bedroom, and now I've found it again on the Net. It's called *Le Château des Pyrénées* and depicts a world in free flight. At least that was the way you and I chose to interpret it. We were agnostics. We couldn't just accept the old idea that everything must have a cause and therefore there must be a 'God' who'd created the world. Certainly we might discuss whether there was something behind what we call the universe. But neither of us believed in any kind of 'revelation' of higher powers. On the other hand we were constantly overawed by our own existence and that of the world.

And Solrun, I have approximately the same feeling about life today. I'll never cease to be amazed that the world exists. Whatever happened up there in the birch copse is, by comparison, a much lesser mystery, in fact insignificant, if you ask me. Circus performers and variety shows will never captivate me in the same way as steppes or rainforest, or the sky's uncountable galaxies and all the billions of light years that separate them.

I'm more concerned, just as you used to be, with the world as a riddle than with riddles in the world. I'm more concerned with the natural than the supernatural. And I feel more wonder for our inscrutable brain than for all these loose anecdotes about the 'extrasensory'.

I don't think it's possible to translate the paradoxes of quantum physics to physics any more than it is to regard 'spiritual' phenomena as thought transference between higher mammals. But that higher mammals exist, and being one myself, fascinates me greatly. In any case, you'd have to search for a long time before you found anybody who was more amazed at his own existence than me. It's quite a claim, but I dare to make it. And so I don't feel stung by your accusation of being short-sighted.

But what's happened to you? Where have you got to?

You say that you now have a sense of certainty about the hereafter, and you proclaim that there is no death. But have you still retained your old ability to delight in every second of the life you're living right here and now? Or has your orientation towards the hereafter gradually displaced that?

Can you still feel 'boundless sorrow' for the fact that life is 'so short, so short'? Those words were once yours. Can your eyes still fill with tears at the thought of words like 'old age' and 'lifetime'? Can you still go into fits of weeping over a sunset? You could also, quite without warning, say wide-eyed and dismayed, One day we'll be gone, Steinn! Or, One day we won't exist any more!

Not all twenty-year-olds have the ability to contemplate the absence of their own existence, at least not with the intensity you could. But we lived together with that as an almost daily reference. Wasn't that why we were constantly embarking on the wildest stunts? After a time I no longer needed to ask you why you cried. I knew why, and you knew I knew. So instead I'd suggest that we went off into the forest or to the mountains. We had many such consolation trips to the woods and wilderness. You loved

---

being outdoors. But your love of what you sometimes called Nature was in a sense an unhappy romance, for you knew all the time that one day you'd be disappointed in what you held so dear, and would finally be left to yourself.

That was how it used to be. You went from laughter to tears. Beneath a thin layer of ecstatic existential delight there was always a sorrow lurking in you. In me too. But I think your sorrow was greater than mine. Your enthusiasm and rapture was too.

But to the 'Lingonberry Woman'. I won't try to dismiss her, and it's true that I did break down completely at the time. The resemblance was so striking. How had she managed to follow us?

Just recently when my hand shook, it was life itself that was trembling. Thirty years had passed, and now as we two walked there again, it suddenly struck me with such vividness what it had been like to be really young, but also what it had been like to be us. Then something happened up there on the birch slope, some accursed thing, that suddenly tore us away from one another.

When I took your hand it certainly had something to do with the birch wood that we'd soon be passing again. I recalled the jolt it had given us all those years before. I remember how terror-stricken we'd been, and I don't deny that once more I felt a shudder or wave of fear. But it wasn't a dread of seeing some ghost again. Dread can also

---

41

be the fear of being overtaken by one's own insanity. Or of the other's. Fear is infectious. Insanity is too.

You weren't yourself again after that. In the weeks that followed it sometimes happened that I was frightened of being in the same room with you. I just held my breath and hoped that you would return to your old self. But before that could happen you took a few of your things and left. For years afterwards I longed for you. I thought you might ring the doorbell at any moment. At night I'd remember that you might also let yourself into the flat while I was sleeping, because you'd never returned the key. I lay in the wide double bed and yearned for you, but I was worried too: you might return before you'd become the old Solrun I'd known, and after some years I had a mortise lock put on the door.

The 'Lingonberry Woman' remains one of the enigmatic events in my life. But we were so young at the time. And besides it was more than thirty years ago and now I don't know what to think any more.

☐ Yes, Steinn.

☐ What do you mean?

☐ He's standing there again! I can't concentrate. I can't think back thirty years while he's standing on that ladder constantly dipping his brush into a pot of green paint. Is it *really* necessary to put on two coats? Aren't you at least supposed to leave a day in between so that the first coat is completely dry?

☐ Well, do something else then. I'll be here for a couple of hours yet.

☐ I've got myself a glass of apple juice with four cubes of ice in it, and now the legs and the ladder have gone, thank goodness. He won't come back and apply a third coat, surely?

Agnostics. We were living puppets! Do you remember? We went around the whole time with a magical sense of life, and it was a sense of life we felt was ours alone. We were outsiders: we created an enchanted outpost for ourselves that gave us the opportunity to look askance at everything; it was as if we'd founded our own religion. That's what we said, that we'd founded our own religion.

But we weren't just wrapped up in each other, for a time we carried on a certain amount of missionary activity. Do you remember all the Saturdays we rushed into town with a bag full of small, leaflet-like pieces of paper which we handed out to our fellow human beings? We'd spent the previous evening tapping out short messages on an old typewriter. IMPORTANT COMMUNICATION TO ALL INHABITANTS

43

OF THIS CITY: THE WORLD IS HAPPENING NOW! We'd write the same message several thousand times, then cut them up carefully and fold them and get the tram to the National Theatre. There we'd take up position either in the gardens of Studenterlunden or in front of the stairs to the tube station and hand out our small gems of thought in an attempt to awaken parts of the city from what we thought was its spiritual lethargy. We were high-spirited. We were greeted with lots of friendly smiles, but also with a surprising number of exclamations of irritation. Some people feel discommoded at being reminded that they exist.

Not only this, but it wasn't politically correct at the start of the 70s to indulge in idle speculation about existence. Many on the left thought it was counter-revolutionary to point out that the universe is a riddle. The important thing wasn't to understand the world, but to change it.

We'd had the idea for the little messages from those silly Christmas cracker jokes, and I think our original idea was to have some sort of mock Christmas festivity at a student party. Do you remember? We also dreamt of putting together an alternative procession, on 2 May for example. We didn't get much further than writing some of the slogans, and here we did actually have some precedents. In the student uprising in Paris they'd had graffiti like POWER TO THE IMAGINATION! and DEATH IS COUNTER-REVOLUTIONARY on the walls of the Sorbonne. We imagined an entire procession of such slogans. You were so inventive, Steinn.

We used to do the rounds of galleries and concerts – not so much for the art or music, but to look at all the living puppets. We called all this a magic theatre – it was after we'd read Hermann Hesse's *Steppenwolf*. Or sometimes we'd sit in a café and study certain specimens minutely. Each and every one of them was like a small, self-contained universe. We called them souls too, didn't we? I'm sure we did. We weren't watching *mechanical* puppets. They were *living* puppets. That was what we said. Can you remember how we'd sit in some corner of a café and weave complex stories around them? Some of these 'spirits' might be taken home and elaborated on in the days that followed. We gave them names and conjured up entire biographies for them. And so we built up a whole pantheon of fictitious references. An important element in our religion was its almost unbridled worship of humanity.

Then we hung the Magritte poster on the bedroom wall. I think we bought it at the Henie Onstad Art Centre at Hovikodden.

And talking of bedrooms, we could go to bed in the middle of the day, often with a bottle of 'champagne' and two kitchen glasses on the bedside table. We could sit for hours reading aloud to each other. We read Stein Mehren and Olaf Bull – we allowed ourselves those, even though

45

so-called mainstream poets were quite taboo at the time. But we read Jan Erik Vold as well, absolutely everything he wrote. Not to mention *Crime and Punishment* and *The Magic Mountain*. A whole novel could be one of these bed and champagne projects. Our champagne was actually Golden Power. It was cheap and sweet, but it was strong too, hence the name.

We thought it was marvellous to be bodies of flesh and blood. It was so beautiful to be man and woman, we enjoyed it. But in our corporeal happiness there was also a reminder that we were mortal. Autumn begins in spring, we proclaimed. We were in our mid-twenties, but confided to each other that we thought we'd already begun to be old.

Life was a miracle, and it was clear to us that it was something we had to celebrate constantly. It might be with a spontaneous nocturnal walk in the forests around Oslo or with an equally spontaneous car trip. Let's go to Skåne, you'd say. Five minutes later we'd be sitting in the car and on our way. Neither of us had been there before, and we hadn't a clue where we'd be staying.

Do you remember when we arrived at the Lundgren Sisters' open-air tea room in Sweden? We hadn't slept, and we just laughed and laughed. Later we fell asleep in the grass. In the end we were woken by a cow, and if she hadn't turned up we'd have been woken up a few seconds later by ants. We leapt around like lunatics trying to brush the things off us, but they weren't just outside our clothes, but also between them and inside as well. You were so furious at what you called *Swedish* ants. You took them as a personal insult.

The impulse to ski across the Jostedalsbreen glacier was one such escapade, which you've just called a stunt. It was a day in May more than thirty years ago. We're going to ski across Jostedalsbreen! you announced one afternoon, and that was like an order because we had a sort of mutual agreement that the other person had to obey any such whims without demurring. It only took us a few minutes to pack and then we were off. We could spend the night somewhere in the mountains or in Lærdal, or we could sleep in the car. We were wild and uncompromising. When we got to the fjord the idea was to go straight up to the glacier with our skis on our shoulders. We'd heard of a stone hut we could spend the night in if it was too late to set out on skis. Neither of us had any glacier training, and so from that point of view it was totally irresponsible. But it was a trip that never materialised. For the first time something held us back – you know what I'm referring to – and we stayed a whole week at the hotel before we turned back with our tails between our legs. It wasn't cheap – there were no concessions for students. But we had more on our minds than lack of money, and we did have a chequebook.

*

While writing this I'd like to stress that I have precisely the same enchanted view of life today. 'But have you still retained your old ability to delight in every second of the life you're living right here and now?' you ask, and the answer is yes.

But a lot has changed, because there's something extra now, an entirely new dimension really. You ask, 'Can you still feel boundless sorrow for the fact that life is so short, so short? Can your eyes still fill with tears at the thought of words like old age and lifetime?' And I can now answer with a liberated no. I don't cry any more. In relation to what lies ahead of me, I now live in a state of ... tranquillity.

I still derive great joy from my physical self, if not quite as intensely as in the old days. But now I live with my body as a shell, and therefore as something external and unimportant. It's not something I'll be burdened with for much longer. I'm now convinced that what I call *me* will survive the death of my body. I no longer feel that it's my body that *is* me. It's no more 'me' or 'mine' than those old dresses in the wardrobe. I won't be taking those either. Nor the washing machine. Nor the car, nor my debit card.

I'll willingly tell you more about this – more than willingly. I read the Bible a lot these days, not just parapsychology. For me, the one doesn't preclude the other, and perhaps that chimes with your exclusion of both?

But now I put it to you: what do you believe in today? I know your background beliefs, but has something new entered your life as well?

Thanks for your last mail. You were a little less cocksure then than you've been in some of your other correspondence. Your hands were reaching out a bit. But they were empty, Steinn. I have such a craving to put something wonderful into them. One day I'd so love to try to give you a vivid, shimmering proof that there is no death. Just wait. I'll do it one day! Until then, I'm grateful that you at least want to open this channel more than thirty years after it closed to us.

It was awful to read that you were frightened of me. You never said that. I thought you just shut yourself away, and that I was boring you with my new notions.

But despite all this we owe it to one another to keep faith with what we were and what we had before you-know-what happened, and before you think I went crazy. I never did go crazy, but what happened was dramatic enough. I converted suddenly from one philosophy of life to another. The break was especially dramatic because the congregation I left only had two members.

But you remember all the rest of it? You remember our adventures! I think you remember what you want.

☐ Of course I remember, and I've often thought back to

the five years we lived together as the very core of my life.

We decided to walk to Trondheim. And we walked! We decided to sail on Lake Mjøsa. So we sailed. We sat in the Kunstnernes Hus gallery café and got the itch to cycle to Stockholm. So we went home and slept for a few hours. Then we cycled to Stockholm.

The maddest thing we did was that exploit on the Hardangervidda plateau. We'd got the idea that we wanted to try to live like people in the Stone Age for a few weeks. We took the train to the mountains, and made our home on a mountainside a few kilometres south-west of Haugastøl, on a cave-shaped ledge under a slab of rock. We took warm clothes and blankets with us. We had two large packets of sandwiches so we'd have something to eat for the first few hours while we made camp, and for safety's sake we'd brought along various crispbreads and biscuits as emergency rations. We had one cooking pot, a reel of fishing line, a hunting knife and two boxes of matches. And that was the lot. Or rather – and this was the only real anachronism – you had also brought along a blister pack of contraceptive pills. The pack also served as a calendar, as we didn't have any other way of counting the days. For the first twenty-four hours we lived mainly on berries – crowberries, cloudberries and bilberries – and we fortified ourselves with hot juniper tea. Next day we found some bird bones which we could turn into fishing tackle; we dug for worms, and from then on we caught trout which we fried on a piece of slate. We hoped to catch a hare or a grouse. But the hares were too fast and the grouse always took off just as we leapt on them. Our hunger for meat grew more and more, and when we caught sight of a flock of wild reindeer, we shifted some boulders and dug out a pit which we covered with dwarf birch, lichen and moss. We saw nothing more of the reindeer, but eventually a lamb fell into the pit, which we slaughtered without an iota of sentimentality, skinned and survived on for several days. We fashioned fishing hooks and kitchen implements from the bones, and I scraped away at an ornament which I threaded on to a strong plant stalk and hung round your neck. We also had the lamb's fleece. This was a great boon, as the days were getting shorter, and one morning there was frost on the ground. That was when we packed up, and it was with a sense of triumph. You only had four pills left in your pack, so we'd lived like troglodytes for seventeen days. And we'd done a good job of concealing ourselves too, because we hadn't seen a living soul during all that time. We'd shown each other that we could survive like Stone Age people. But it was also wonderful to go home to a shower, a double bed and a bottle of Golden Power. We hardly got out of bed for a day and a half. We were stiff. We'd got jet lag. It was as if we'd been time-travelling for thousands of years.

———

☐ It's funny to think back on, and the kernel of *my* life was perhaps encompassed in the seventeen days we isolated ourselves from the rest of the world and were together up in the mountains beneath the sky, just you and me. But what do you think about today? What do you *believe* in?

Well, perhaps that question is a bit vague. But let's play a little game. You're leaning professorially back in your university study bored to death, and I'm a student who knocks at your door. You invite me in – you're delighted to have a visitor – and I say, What you're teaching us is all extremely fascinating, professor, but what do *you* believe yourself about the things you don't know the answers to? You're flattered by this direct and essentially highly personal question from your favourite female student and so you embark on a mini-lecture. Off you go, Steinn! This is the mini-lecture I'm waiting for. (But don't make it too long. I see it's going to be a barbecue evening again, and so I'll have to make a salad at least.)

☐ You're joking! How could I resist such a temptation?

☐ Well, just succumb to it.

☐ In that case I can simply continue where I left off, because I believe we're descended from just such Stone

---

52

Age people. Who didn't fill themselves with contra-
ceptives. In common with them we belong to the species
Homo sapiens, which is a direct descendant of *Homo
erectus*, which again is descended from *Homo habilis* and
then back to *Australopithecus africanus.*

We're primates, Solrun. You remember? If we go back a
few million years, we share the same origins as chim-
panzees and gorillas. But you know all this. We talked
about it. It was part of the nerve behind our intense feeling
for life, behind our feeling of being a part of nature. Next,
we're mammals, in common with the hares and reindeer
on Hardangervidda, and this class of vertebrates developed
a couple of hundred million years ago from certain
mammal-like reptiles, the so-called therapsids.

But why look back? It's like moving against the current.
Wouldn't it be better to position ourselves at the other end
and take part in the breakneck journey right from the
beginning? I'll settle for a brief overview.

This intensely mysterious universe is about 13.7 billion
years old, according to the latest calculations. At that time
something called the *big bang* occurred. How? Why? Don't
ask me. And don't ask anyone else either, because nobody
knows. But in a fraction of a second a huge release of
energy occurred and came together as protons and neutrons as well as electrons and other so-called leptons. As
the universe cooled, the light elements emerged, and, over

time, so did stars and planets, galaxies and galaxy clusters. Our own solar system and planet are 4.6 billion years old, so roughly a third of the age of the universe, and we've gradually gained a degree of insight into the earth's history and development.

The very first primitive life forms began here three or four billion years ago, regardless of whether they developed here from the ground up – on location, if you like – or if the building blocks of life (we can call them prebiotic material) came from far away as the result of comet or asteroid strikes. What is certain, however, is that at that time the planet had no oxygen in its atmosphere, and so in the beginning there wasn't any protective ozone layer round our planet either. These were both important prerequisites in encouraging the formation of the macromolecules of life, and here we come to an interesting paradox. The conditions necessary for life to flourish (like an oxygen-rich atmosphere and a defensive ozone layer) must be absent for life to begin. So the first living cells presumably evolved in the sea, and perhaps at great depths. Liberated oxygen and an ozone layer are the results of photosynthesis – therefore of life itself – and a necessary basis for higher organisms to exist here. But new life cannot evolve again. The overwhelming probability is that all life on this planet is precisely the same age.

Only when photosynthesising organisms evolved in the earliest aeon of the earth's history, or in what we call the

Precambrian period, were the conditions right for higher organisms such as plants and animals. In the Cambrian period (from 543 to 510 million years ago), came the first molluscs and arthropods, and in the Ordovician period (from 510 to 440 million years ago) the first vertebrates. An internal skeleton gave life entirely new possibilities, and it was the representatives of a small branch of this line of animals which, half a billion years later, blasted into space and began researching our cosmic beginnings.

During the Silurian period (from 440 to 409 million years ago) the first terrestrial plants appeared, as did the first land animals, the earliest of which were the scorpions. They were arthropods, from the class Arachnida, and were the first to scramble on to dry land. But as early as the late Devonian period (from 409 to 354 million years ago) amphibians were crawling ashore, particularly the laby-rinthodonts, descendants of one of the so-called lobe-finned fish, and in the Carboniferous period (from 354 to 290 million years ago) land vertebrates developed very rapidly, with a richly diversified family of amphibians and gradually reptiles as well, a development that continued into the Permian period (from 290 to 245 million years ago). Especially characteristic of this period was the number of reptiles adapting to a drier climate, and it was in this epoch that the first therapsids evolved, the reptilian order from which all mammals are descended.

The Triassic period (from 245 to 206 million years ago)

---

saw the first mammals and the first dinosaurs. Dinosaurs dominated life on dry land from the end of the Triassic, throughout all of the Jurassic period (from 206 to 144 million years ago) until a global catastrophe, presumably a meteorite strike in Yucatán on the Gulf of Mexico, exterminated the last dinosaurs at the end of the Cretaceous period (from 144 to 65 million years ago). But that wasn't quite the end of the dinosaurs. Everything points to the fact that the grouse you and I tried to catch on the Hardanger plateau are actually direct descendants of a particular family of dinosaurs, a provenance they share with all other birds. Palaeontologists often joke that birds *are* dinosaurs.

But you and I and all other primates are related to some shrew-like insectivores which came scuttling out 65 million years ago as soon as the carnivorous dinosaurs' tyranny was over. Don't you remember us joking about it? That we were shrews!

Throughout the Tertiary period (from 65 to 1.8 million years ago) our mammalian order, the primates, was undergoing a rapid evolution, and our own great-great-grandfather *Australopithecus* or 'next to man', whom I've already mentioned, turns up on the threshold of the Quaternary period (from 1.8 million years ago), which is our own geological period.

This is what I believe in! I believe in the knowledge that cosmology and astrophysics give us, and I believe in what biology and palaeontology are able to tell us about the development of life on earth. I believe absolutely and completely in the philosophy of the natural sciences. It's changing all the time: research takes two steps forward and one to the side, or one step forward and two to the side. But I believe in natural laws, and in the final analysis that means the laws of physics and mathematics.

I believe in what *exists*. I believe in facts. We don't yet know about everything, and we don't understand everything – our knowledge is full of holes. But we know and comprehend a great deal more than our ancestors.

Don't you think it's really impressive just how much insight we've gained during just the last century? We can begin our century with Einstein's special theory of relativity in 1905. Behind the equation $E = mc^2$ lies an almost unbelievably profound understanding of the nature of the universe. Energy can be turned into mass, and mass into energy. In the 1920s Hubble discovered cosmic red shift and was able to determine that the galaxies are moving away from each other at a speed which is proportional to their distance. This must be one of the century's great breakthroughs, because it brought with it the knowledge that the universe is expanding and that its origin was the big bang, a theory which in many ways has been confirmed since, not least by the detection of cosmic background radiation, showing us that the universe is still hot after the enormous explosion 13.7 billion years ago. In 1990 the great space telescope – named after Hubble – was put into orbit round the earth and, after necessary repairs and adjustments, it's been able to give us extremely important pictures many billions of light years out into the universe, and thus just as many billions of years back into its history. For looking out into the universe is the same as looking back in time. Today there isn't much to stop us from looking right back to the beginning of the universe, although it isn't possible to see further back than 300,000 years after the big bang. Throughout the century biochemistry and our understanding of what life is has also been developing at breakneck speed. One important moment was Crick and Watson's description of the intertwined spiral of the DNA molecule in 1953. Another was the mapping of the human genome, the roughly three billion base pairs that the human genome consists of. The map was complete by the end of the century. The next milestone in our understanding of the universe and the nature of matter will be the world's largest physics experiment at CERN sometime in the course of 2008. An entirely new particle accelerator will then come into use, the aim of which is to investigate which elementary particles the universe was composed of 0.000,000,000,001 of a second after the big bang. Perhaps we'll be able to stop complaining about man's imperfect understanding the day we comprehend the history of this universe right back to its first microscopic fraction of a second.

———

*

It often used to be said that to discuss the big questions about the origins of the world or the essence of life was as pointless as discussing the dark side of the moon, because the moon always shows us the same aspect. But today this idea is both naive and invalid as – after the moon journeys – we can now find detailed photographs of its dark side in any bookshop.

☐ I'm impressed. No, I'm being sarcastic.

You remind me of a small boy who can't answer the question he's been asked and instead starts talking about something entirely different. I asked what you believe now about the miracle of the world, not what you think you and the rest of humanity know.

Surely you don't think *that* was what our sweet little student came into your study to ask you about? She hardly wanted to use you as a reference book.

I don't have any desire to distance myself from your interpretation of astronomy, palaeontology or scientific history. So you're welcome to them. But you're simply rehearsing a litany of facts. This means you're not answering anything. You have no theories about how or why everything happened. You just reflect the world as it appears to us all.

You don't say a word about the most mysterious thing of all – and perhaps also the most essential – that we're coruscating spirits as well. Each and every one of us is a soul in the universe. Wasn't *that* what we saw in the 'puppets' back then?

Imagine a child going to its mother and asking, Who am I? Or, What is a human being? And the mother picking up a knife and starting to cut into the child's flesh so that she can answer the questions better.

But there was one passage I did read several times. You write: 'This intensely mysterious universe is about 13.7 billion years old according to the latest calculations. At that time something called the big bang occurred. How? Why? Don't ask me. And don't ask anyone else either, because nobody knows ...'

It was on this scintillating outer edge that we stood back then. We gave way to an ecstatic agnosticism about all that was 'intensely mysterious'. Perhaps it was this ardour that gave us the energy to live for seventeen days as cavemen. We were giddy with wonder and had to investigate absolutely everything. At least the answer to what it was like to live like Stone Age people was within our grasp.

But the distance between us today need not be so very great. The difference is perhaps simply that what you call the 'big bang' is what I call the moment of creation, or as it says in the third verse of Genesis, 'God said, "Let there be light", and there was light.'

———

What you brush aside as a 'release of energy' is for me an act of creation, and I have to say that from my point of view it seems almost unbelievably dreary to get as close as 0.000,000,000,001 of a second to the creative hand of God without sensing even the vaguest hint of the divine presence. In my opinion it shows a certain lack of sensitivity.

But now I'll give you another chance. What do you *believe*? I mean about the things we don't know.

☐ Are you deleting?

☐ What?

☐ Have you remembered to delete my emails before answering them?

☐ Yes . . .

☐ You just seem to be able to remember what I wrote so well. Like that 'passage' you just quoted. You put quotation marks around it, and as far as I could tell, you quoted me word for word.

☐ You're being very sweet. I've always had a marvellous memory. I *do* have certain 'gifts' . . .

———

☐ Well?

☐ But Jonas and Niels Petter have just lit the barbecue, and I've got to go and make a salad. I've just this moment noticed that Jonas has outgrown his father. All in all I see I'm going to be tied up for the rest of this evening. But what about tomorrow?

☐ I'll have plenty of time then. Enjoy your family evening!

☐ And I hope you'll have a nice time with that witty father-in-law of yours.

III

☐ Good morning! Is anyone there?

☐ You sent half an hour ago. But now I'm in front of my screen and online.

☐ It's quite unbelievable out here. There's not a breath of wind, and it's already pleasantly warm. I've carried my laptop out into the sun and am sitting at the table out in the little garden where Grandma used to tend her flowers and hum her little refrain: Oh, how nice that Steinn is.

Coming from the west of the country does this to you. We don't pass up a warm summer's day. In honour of the sun and my surroundings I've put on a yellow summer dress with some fine cherry appliqué, and I've actually got a small bowl of cherries in front of me on the table, next to my laptop. I bought them down on the quay at Eide's Groceries.

And you?

☐ I think I mentioned that we're in Nordberg, not far from where you and I used to live, in fact, and I remember that on a couple of occasions we walked past the house where I now live at the top of Kongleveien, but you'll obviously have forgotten all the street names in a district you won't have set foot in for more than thirty years.

I'm sitting on a glassed-in veranda looking down on a south-facing garden. It's almost like sitting outside, because I've opened two large windows, and the occasional bumblebee flies in, but then it flies out again a few moments later. Berit wanted to fill it with flowers, but I managed to persuade her that we have more than enough flowers out in the garden, but in return I've had to put up with the veranda being stuffed full of plants all winter, and then there aren't any bumblebees or wasps flying in through open windows. I'm describing a typical marital compromise. The least you can do is meet halfway and agree to such arrangements.

Berit has just returned to work after the holidays. Perhaps I told you that she's an eye specialist and works at Ullevål Hospital. Ine and Norunn are gadding about as usual, they're as giddy as the summer itself, and so I'm alone in the house.

☐ I remember Kongleveien well and how we use to stroll about round there. We'd walk to Berg station, and occasionally right down to the university. It was more than just a couple of times, Steinn. And besides I've paid a flying visit to Kringsjå almost every time I've been in Oslo. I lived up there for five years, don't forget, and those were important years. It used to be my home, and to this day I still do a circuit or two of Lake Sognsvann. It's not a restricted area, is it?

☐ Of course not. It's just nice to know that you've been here in the interim.

☐ But I've never met you. At Lake Sognsvann, I mean.

☐ Well, there you are.

☐ There you are what?

☐ Chance. It doesn't always work.

☐ Maybe the Great Reunion was to be saved until we were back on that old veranda again ...

☐ You're being funny. But when you walk round the lake, do you go clockwise or anticlockwise?

☐ Anticlockwise, Steinn. We always used to.

☐ And I'm as conservative as you are. So I might have

been walking fifty or a hundred metres behind you. But now I've started jogging, so next time I may catch you up.

☐ At the moment I'm more interested in forming a picture of you sitting at your computer on a glassed-in veranda in Nordberg. I noted the bumblebee that just paid you a visit, so thanks for that. But I need a few more details so that I can completely forget that in reality we're two ferry crossings and 600 kilometres apart. Isn't there anything else you can describe?

☐ Well, I'm wearing a white T-shirt and khaki shorts and have nothing on my feet. In front of me on a tiny table, which is really only a stand, I've got just enough room for a laptop, but there's a double espresso and a glass of mineral water on the window ledge. I'm sitting on a bar stool, and where that came from I can't remember. Outside it's already nearly 25 degrees, and in the garden, which is bounded by a thuja hedge, I can see a specimen tree of unripe grey pears and also two plum trees with almost ripe violet-blue plums, and I've got a feeling the species is called Herman. A thick bouquet of yellow loosestrife is bursting from round an old sundial – they flower nearly all summer – and striding along next to the shingle path are some clusters of white and red astilbes – they flower late but they last, like small, suggestive pillars, until well into the autumn.

———

Is that sufficient compensation for the two ferry journeys and 600 kilometres?

□ That's a great help, because now I can see you. But shorts? You never used to wear them. You generally wore corduroy trousers, sometimes brown, sometimes beige and sometimes bright red. So *something* has changed.

You can begin talking to me now, Steinn. I'm sitting here.

□ Begin talking to you?

□ You're being given a second chance to say what you believe about those things you can't explain.

□ Ah, yes. I think you put roughly the same question to me out there, and I can't recall exactly what I said. But when you'd both left the Book Town that Wednesday, I spent a long time walking in the garden and pondering yet again why we'd left each other. It was because of just such questions of belief. As I'd been reminded of the 'Lingonberry Woman', I tried to bring to mind all the conversations we'd had about such things before that sudden silence descended on us and everything fell apart.

I feel a bit apprehensive about dredging it up again. Because you're right about me sitting in the bedroom practically chain-smoking that last evening and night,

I was in such despair. We couldn't talk to each other any more. We could hardly stay in the same room together. When I lay down sometime towards dawn, there was only one cigarette left in the pack of twenty – I remember it well, because I lit it sitting on the edge of the bed when I got up an hour later. Before I'd got halfway through it, I stubbed it out and went into the living room, and there you were sitting on the edge of the sofa, and you had a cigarette too.

Steinn, was all you said, but there was something in your eyes and I nodded.

I knew you were going to leave that day. And you knew that I knew. I didn't try to stop you.

Now you return after more than thirty years and ask me what I believe in? Perhaps you'll find this disappointing, but I'm not sure I have any sort of personal 'belief' in anything. So it's easier for me to define what I don't believe in.

☐ I think you're just being difficult now. So what is it you *don't* believe in?

☐ I can put it in one word. I don't believe in any kind of *revelation*. Apart from that there's plenty to wonder at, and a whole mass of things we don't know. There's an almost limitless field of things one can believe and doubt.

☐ Yes?

☐ We use the word 'believe' in many different contexts. We may believe that Manchester United will win against Liverpool, or we can believe the weather will be fine tomorrow. By this we mean that we think one thing is more likely than another. Perhaps it *is* more likely that Manchester United will win Sunday's football match, and perhaps there *are* signs that the weather tomorrow will be fine. But these aren't the things we're discussing here.

Then there is another category of questions of belief which we can also leave alone for the moment – I'm thinking particularly of a question you've already touched on, whether what we call the big bang happened on its own, or whether it was the result of a divine act of creation. This is a question nobody can answer definitively; it's a typical faith question, and I have great respect for the notion that the big bang may have been one of God's miracles, even though the word or term 'God' is much too loaded with human concepts for me to use myself. In the same category there is also, in my opinion, another question that concerns you, that is whether there is something within us, a 'soul' or 'spirit', which survives death. Personally, I think it's unlikely that there's anything in me that will survive what I am today, but that isn't because I think such a belief is incompatible with science, even though it might be said to inhabit a grey area. But I wouldn't want to dismiss the belief in an existence after this one – much less rob you of it – on any scientific grounds.

☐ That's great. But?

☐ But I don't believe that any 'supernatural' powers constantly interpose themselves in our lives and 'appear' to us. I should have been much clearer about all this then, because it wasn't your sudden conviction about a life after this one that I reacted to, but that you linked such notions to the idea that the 'Lingonberry Woman' was a manifestation from the hereafter. And as you've already pointed out, she was something we'd experienced together. Even though I instantly connected her with what we'd seen up by that lake in the mountains, I couldn't believe she'd died there and had now returned to visit us from 'the other side'.

☐ I understand. But carry on, Steinn. At the moment I want to try to understand you fully, then when it's my turn, I'll put my own point of view across. Just spit it right out; I can take it.

☐ Well then, here it is. I don't believe there has ever been an instance in all of human history when gods or angels, spirits or ancestors, sprites or ghosts appeared, or by some other means announced themselves, to any person or race, and the reason is the simplest of all reasons: namely that such things don't exist.

☐ Now I've eaten five cherries. I'm putting the stones on the table in front of me, so it's easy to keep count.

There are rumours that Eide's Groceries will be closing after being a family business since 1883. There are shops at Nåra and in Ytrøygrend, and the island only has a permanent population of a couple of hundred. But I think it would sad if we lost the shop out here on the headland. Of course, you can drive or bike to Nåra and shop there, but when a small community like Kolgrov loses its shop, the entire fabric of the place begins to unravel, at least in the wintertime when the summer visitors aren't here.

Do you remember all our cycle trips that summer? I know you do. Every evening we had to go out to Søndre Hjønnevåg and look out at the sea and the sunset, and then we had to bathe in all the tarns on the way home.

But carry on, Steinn. I'm not as fragile as you think. You were saying that you don't believe in supernatural forces . . .

☐ Well, as you're asking, here is my Galileo telescope. Try to envisage that absolutely all ideas about 'supernatural' phenomena are purely human notions which have no basis whatsoever other than in man himself. There, to make up for it, they find very fertile soil. I think that there are three significant factors: our surfeit of imagination, our innate need to search for hidden meanings even where no such meanings exist, and lastly our congenital yearning for a brand new existence after this one, I mean a life after death.

This cocktail of human nature has proved uncommonly productive. In absolutely every age – and in every society and culture – human beings have fostered raft after raft of concepts concerning supernatural beings like nature spirits, ancestors, gods, giants, angels or demons.

☐ You really are so sure of yourself, aren't you?

☐ Take the teeming life of our imaginations for a start. Everybody dreams, so nobody can defend themselves completely from hallucinations, and in certain situations the same thing can also happen when we're awake. We think we see and feel things without the things we're perceiving having any basis in reality. Who hasn't asked themselves if this or that memory is something they've really experienced, or if it's just something they've been told or thought about, dreamt or imagined?

I've met people myself who claim they've seen 'fairies'. But our heads are perpetually so crammed with sensual impressions that it's hardly surprising they boil over occasionally, I mean that small disturbances occur, things we generally call illusions or chimeras.

The leap from these very natural attacks of sensual distraction to what we call religious truths occurs when we permit our own, or other people's, imaginings to attain the status of objective, existing beings, independent of our own consciousness or that of others. I'm thinking of everything from nature spirits, the great throng of mystical figures we meet in old national religions, to the more elevated or intellectualised concepts we are presented with in the great universal religions, the notion, for example, of an all-powerful God revealing himself to human beings on earth, i.e. on our planet in the Milky Way.

I ought here to make an important distinction, however. As well as a few ethical ideals, all religions contain a cornucopia of human experience, which can be very valuable in itself. And as I've said, it isn't people's *religiousness* I want to cast doubt on. The limit is only reached for me when I hear or read of people who invoke personal contact with an almighty God, who has spoken to them or manifested himself to them with a specific message which everyone else must obey. Millions of people live on this earth believing that God is talking to them – and telling them what to do – in an entirely personal way. Millions and millions of people are also convinced that an all-powerful God controls every least thing that happens here, whether it's a tsunami, a nuclear war or a mosquito bite.

☐ Or a battery running down in a laptop out here in the

mouth of the fjord. I'll try to solve the problem. Just go on writing. At the moment I haven't got the battery power to engage in a lengthy discussion with you, and I'm not going inside in this weather.

☐ Shall I just continue?

☐ Yes, Steinn. It will be my turn next, and I hope you're psychologically prepared for it. Maybe it'll be my job to rake around in what we experienced back then. I don't know how much you remember. But carry on.

☐ I can't say I'm looking forward to what you'll be raking around in, but providing we're deleting I'll accept your conditions, and so I'll go on.

We've looked a little at what we might call the religious solution. But human nature doesn't change, and you know I've never believed in parapsychology's menu of 'paranormal' or 'extrasensory' phenomena either. Here I'm not only thinking of spiritualist seances and all the variations of spirit conjuring in Victorian drawing rooms. That sort of duplication of reality has fallen out of fashion a bit. I'm thinking of modern concepts of telepathy and clairvoyance, psychokinesis and ghosts. Ancient ideas about angels and 'guardians' have also enjoyed a strong resurgence over the past few years. But these also come down to a type of revelational belief related to concepts about the possibility of getting in contact with certain transcendental or extrasensory forces. Not so long ago there was a bit of a stir when 38 per cent of the Norwegian population stated that they thought it possible for human beings to communicate with angels.

In this list of pseudo-phenomena I also include all forms of prophecy, as these too are based on the existence of a preordained destiny which can be exposed or revealed using certain techniques, especially through the mediation of well-paid fortune-tellers. We're talking here about an entire industry, the turnover of which is probably as big as that of the sex trade. Pornography and occultism are presumably equally saleable commodities, even though one is to do with something eminently natural, and the other with something supernatural.

The only thing this so-called parapsychology can really do, in my opinion, is to map a landscape that doesn't exist – I mean a fanciful or imagined landscape. Now this doesn't mean that all parapsychological literature is worthless. As a description of the sort of notions that exist in the broad swathe of the population, such literature can make interesting reading on a par with the history of religion, folklore and other cultural disciplines. We don't consider fairy tales to be worthless, and we're clearly glad that Snorri collected much of the old Norse and Germanic mythology before it was forgotten.

---

*

I've got more to say, but I'm open to comments along the way, so I'm sending you these tentative thoughts before your battery goes completely flat.

...

I'm not getting any reply from you, so you've probably got battery problems already. For now, I mean until you send me an answer, I'll continue with my trifling analysis.

By rejecting all ideas of supernatural or extrasensory phenomena, I'm simultaneously adopting a sceptical attitude to all similar concepts within the established religions. In my view these are two sides of the same coin, and I wonder if it's especially useful to make any formal distinction between revelational religions on the one hand and more unbridled or undogmatic tinkering with notions of 'supernatural phenomena' on the other. In contrast to parapsychology's burgeoning flora of anecdotes about 'supernatural' occurrences, the corresponding narratives have congealed into dogma in the great world religions, and live on within the framework of a structured and well organised faith in the intervention of divine powers.

How is it even possible to make a distinction between faith and superstition? One person's faith is another person's superstition – and vice versa. The scales of justice have two pans.

I can't quite see the difference between speaking in tongues and the spiritualist's fraternising with spirits. Isn't the person speaking in tongues also a 'medium'? I can't see any difference between religious prophecies and an ever-youthful panoply of necromantic arts. Whether we label the occurrences as 'miracles' or psychokinesis, 'ascension' or levitation is all the same to me, because in each case it concerns a suspension of all natural laws.

The very notion that 'the supernatural' in certain rare cases is revealed to us, is something that superstition, parapsychology and the world religions have in common – in contrast to what we call a naturalistic or scientific world view. You use the word apparition, but that means almost the same thing as 'revelation'.

One important motivation for the parapsychological research you referred to was precisely that it attempted to find a scientific foundation for the belief in a life after this one, something that gathered momentum as Darwinism and freethinking began to threaten the traditional religions. You mention the Rhines, and I've done a little research. The incentive for this couple as well as the other pioneers of experimental parapsychology was to demonstrate the immortality of the soul. If they could only manage to provide watertight proof that telepathy was a genuine phenomenon, it would be easier to defend the belief that human beings have an eternal soul, a 'free' soul, which only inhabits the brain temporarily and without being inextricably linked to it. But no such irrefutable proof has yet been found.

I'm sending again. But are you receiving me?

☐ I am indeed! I found an old extension lead in the tool shed, and now I'm getting power from the house. Attached by its long red lead, my laptop resembles a satellite of the island's electrical system. So at the moment it's physically linked to the house and its surroundings, *but not inextricably*.

We've just got a wireless router here, and it covers the whole of the small garden. Without any plugs or leads at all I can sit here and communicate with the entire world.

So just try imagining that human beings aren't the only ones who have managed to create such wireless networks ...

☐ You're thinking of telepathy, and maybe also of contact with the spirits of the dead?

☐ I'm thinking of lots of things. But I'd like you to be able to finish what you've got to say first so that I get a chance to understand you. First, you set out your opinions, and

I prod and poke a bit as you go. Then it will be my turn to take the floor with all my opinions.

☐ That's fine. Provided we don't forget the last bit, because I'd like to understand you as well.

☐ I'll have to re-narrate in detail what we actually experienced back then as well, because it's impossible for me to separate the event from my religious identity today. I think you may have forgotten some of it – some of the most important points, I mean – and as I told you, I've got a very good memory.

☐ Isn't that something we can discuss later, if necessary? I mean, whether you really should do that. Whether *we* should do that. After all, we did once promise each other that we'd never rake it up again.

☐ We'll see. This is a process.

When I found the long extension cable and unreeled it into the garden, Ingrid rolled her eyes. I thought you were on holiday, she expostulated. She thinks I'm working on some Teachers' Council stuff or that I'm preparing the French lessons for the next school year – this year I'm doing a few Italian classes as well, by the way. Neither would have been particularly surprising in themselves, as it's barely a week until school begins. But a while ago Niels Petter and Jonas came back from fishing. Niels Petter threw me and the extension cable an almost anxious glance before coming over and stroking my neck while he helped himself to the cherries. He studiously avoided glancing at the computer screen, which isn't all that easy to see anyway in this bright sunlight. I think he knows I'm sitting exchanging emails with someone, and I suspect he's got a hunch it's you. I daren't say what I'm writing or who I'm writing to, and it's as if he doesn't dare ask about it either.

Any news from Nordberg? If something doesn't happen on that glass veranda soon, I'll start worrying that you've dropped out of sight.

☐ I've done almost nothing but sit here and write, wait for replies and read them. You keep on replying immediately after I've sent. Although, to be honest, I've just been to the corner cupboard and poured myself a small glass of Calvados. That espresso was a bit insipid.

☐ Don't go to that corner cupboard again, Steinn. But carry on now. You were saying about parapsychology and the supernatural . . .

☐ That's where we'd got to, yes.

———

James Randi, the famous American magician, has offered a million-dollar prize to the first person who can 'show, under proper observing conditions, evidence of any paranormal, supernatural or occult power'. It's called the One Million Dollar Paranormal Challenge and was set up back in 1964 when Randi offered a thousand dollars from his own pocket to the first person who could demonstrate anything supernatural. Gradually, the prize was supported by others as well and soon the amount had risen to a million dollars. But to this day no one has managed to pass the test.

Well, you can object of course and say that clairvoyants or people with supernatural gifts aren't necessarily greedy for money. But even of the thousands of money-loving charlatans who fill newspaper columns and appear on cheap entertainment channels, hardly any have gone in for the One Million Dollar Paranormal Challenge to snap up the easy money of Randi's prize. Why not? The answer is very simple: because there aren't any clairvoyants or people with 'supernatural' gifts.

Most of those who have stepped up to take on Randi's One Million Dollar Paranormal Challenge, and there have been many of them, have not in fact been professionals from the 'supernatural' business. That group has generally avoided him like the plague; he is, after all, threatening to eradicate their entire industry. (Of course, he'll never succeed, because the world *wants* to be deceived!)

***

Some years ago one of the USA's VIP 'clairvoyants', Sylvia Browne, came head to head with Randi on the TV show *Larry King Live*, and when Randi challenged her to demonstrate her gifts in controlled conditions, she promised on air to allow herself to be tested. That was some years ago now, but she still hasn't turned up to see Randi. Her excuse on one occasion was that she didn't know how to get in touch with him. I think that's pretty rich. It's pretty rich to claim clairvoyant powers and yet be incapable of getting hold of a number in a telephone directory.

The majority of the people who have entered the One Million Dollar Paranormal Challenge have been naive, plausible or mentally disturbed. Randi has had to tighten up the rules constantly so as to avoid running the challenge in a way that might cause danger or harm to the participants. If, for example, a man offers to demonstrate that he has the ability to hurl himself off a ten-storey building without injuring himself, Randi isn't willing to let him try.

But the entire One Million Dollar Paranormal Challenge ought to be superfluous, because if you were clairvoyant, if you had paranormal abilities, there would be many other opportunities for enriching yourself. I've already mentioned roulette, but other typical drawing-room games would provide plenty of scope for profit if you had supernatural powers. But I've never heard of any poker ring throwing out one of the players because he was clairvoyant. What they're concerned about is cheating.

Supernatural powers and hoax. We're speaking now of two ancient bedfellows, assuredly as old as the human race itself.

And James Randi's million dollars remains untouched.

For many people the final bastion of the 'supernatural' has been the experience of meaningful flukes, or of 'non-causal coincidences', what Carl Gustave Jung termed synchronicity. This is something we've already discussed in connection with our reunion out there in the arm of the fjord, and we aren't alone in having such experiences. You might be thinking of someone you haven't thought about for decades, when suddenly you turn a corner and you find yourself face to face with that very individual. Many people experience such chance meetings as the ultimate proof of a supernatural dimension. And it's true: in the moment when this sort of fluke occurs the subject feels a bit giddy and helpless, and that's hardly surprising.

But as we touched on in some of our first emails, what Jung called synchronicity is just pure, simple coincidence in my opinion.

☐ You're so certain the whole time. But not everything that 'is' or that 'happens' can necessarily be tested by scientific methods. I wouldn't find it all that strange if this world's science was only able to demonstrate what was *of* this world.

Can't you let everyone believe what they want? What about the saying, Live and let live?

□ Of course people must be allowed to believe what they want. But when anyone declares that higher authorities have revealed truths to them, we have cause to look a little askance. You know how common it is for individuals or groups to cite a mission or calling from God, whether that mission is aggressive or benign. Others simply complain that they're hearing 'voices' and go to a psychiatrist.

Claims about 'wonders' and 'miracles' have been used throughout history by individuals and entire peoples not merely to cling to position and privilege, but also to instigate oppressive and inhumane acts. We know that religion can inspire people to pious, unselfish and philanthropic deeds. But both history and the daily newspapers show how religious concepts can be misused. Atrocities committed in the name of gods, patriarchs and ancestors have dogged man's history from time immemorial.

Jesus managed to stop a group of men from stoning a woman who'd been caught in the act of adultery. But stoning continues, and in some countries the rapist goes free while the female victim can be sentenced to death by stoning.

Recently a man in a Middle Eastern country was

executed because, amongst other things, he'd allegedly attempted to use witchcraft to drive two people apart. And there was a woman in the same country who was sentenced to decapitation because she'd used witchcraft to make a man impotent. Of course it's an awful thing to make a man impotent. But here it is appropriate to refute the notion that 'sorcery' and 'witchcraft' are real phenomena. Evil exists, but in my opinion it's important to emphasise that the evil committed by people is the work of people themselves, and not that of demons or malevolent spirits.

If we take a broader view, we can see that mankind is still suffused by a belief in sorcery, by contact with ancestors or the dead, and also by the entire gamut of so-called paranormal phenomena. In parts of Africa, Asia and Latin America the belief in witchcraft, black magic and ancestral influence on individual conduct is so pervasive that it dominates the lives of millions of people. But superstition is rife in industrialised countries too. Large sections of the populations of Europe and the USA maintain that they believe in ghosts, in possession by evil spirits, in the possibility of communicating with the dead, as well as in more 'civilised' phenomena such as clairvoyance, telepathy and precognition.

I said that religious concepts can be 'misused', but torture and acts of brutality can also have their roots in religious paradigms. The zeal used against certain enemies, heretics or entire peoples hasn't been without divine precedents. For fundamentalists – and they're found in every corner of the world – everything that is written in ancient holy scripture and revealed scripture can become the norm. Therefore we need ongoing religious criticism. This is no longer directly life-threatening in most countries, but there are still many exceptions, and this makes criticism even more important.

. . .

Are you there, Solrun?

☐   Yes, Steinn. I just have to catch my breath before answering. Just wait a moment.

☐ I'll wait.

☐ I agree with your last point, and I willingly concur in your denunciation of dogmatism and fundamentalism. Although I find a lot to rejoice in and marvel at in the New Testament, I don't believe that God dictated every last syllable of the Bible. One of the key points for me is faith in the risen Christ.

Not long ago Niels Petter got up on his ladder again and

put a *third* coat on the window frames! At the moment he's picking raspberries. It's as if he's keeping watch in the garden just because I'm sitting here writing. Once he asked what I was writing, and I told him the truth. At the moment, I said, I'm sending an email to Steinn.

Have you got more you want to say? Or is the religious criticism over for the time being? I think you've said quite a lot. Enough perhaps?

☐ I've got one final point.

☐ Well, out with it, Steinn! There's no censorship here at least.

☐ Much revelational religion builds on the idea that life in this world is merely a transitional staging post to a heavenly destination. So the conditions in the here and now are of less importance than they would be if there wasn't a greater and more genuine world to come.

As a climatologist I never tire of reminding people that we may only have this one planet to cling to. But many people live with the notion that, in the long run, the planet and the physical means of life here are not that important to nurture because God's judgement and salvation for the faithful is near at hand anyway. So our earthly existence can easily come to be regarded as an intermediate phase,

---

and there are even groups of believers who look forward to a collapse of the biosphere because they see it as an omen of the last days and the Second Coming. It says so in the Bible!

According to a poll carried out for CNN, 59 per cent of Americans believe that the prophecies in Revelation will come to pass, and that the Day of Judgement will take place in accordance with this most fantastic apocalypse. But it doesn't stop there. There are plenty of preachers and pastors who help sow the seeds of international conflict, so that they can actually help *expedite* Jesus' return. Such doomsday Christians may well have influence high up in the White House because, like a species of mole, they always surface during American presidential elections.

I have little fear of such doomsday prophecies, as you know, and I'm sure the same applies to you. But I am terrified of what we call self-fulfilling prophecies. Perhaps there won't be a new heaven and earth. Perhaps there won't be a Last Judgement with redemption for the faithful. Perhaps this earth is the only thing we have, our only home and our only link. In that case, nothing can be more important than our responsibility as stewards of this planet and all the species on it.

□ Of course, Steinn. We should take care of the planet. But I don't think you're silly enough to lay the blame for environmental degradation on believers. I would imagine that many of us who have faith have a greater respect for nature than people who have no belief whatsoever. Can't you see that the mindless over-consumption in large parts of the world is a manifestation of crude materialism? The diametrical opposite of a spiritual orientation, if you ask me. Everything at the moment is being chopped and changed to try to find ways of reducing greenhouse gasses. The only thing nobody dares introduce into the discussion is the potential we have for reducing our enormous consumption, history's most lethal cocktail of jump-in-and-drive and throwaway goods. We live in a historical epoch which our descendants may well end up calling the age of consumer fascism, and I'm convinced that the consumerist ideology of our time can, to a large extent, be seen as a substitute for religion.

☐ Perhaps you're right, and I willingly concede the point. I really haven't got any evidence for maintaining that people who believe in a life after this one are any less willing to be responsible for the planet than those who don't share their beliefs. But I caution against relying on the notion that 'heaven and earth will pass away', and that there's a new world waiting with salvation for the faithful.

☐ There'll soon have to be a bit of a change – at this end anyway. I think the others have long since got fed up with the way I've isolated myself today, and I have to admit

---

that my isolation has been almost demonstrative. Perhaps the long extension cable from the house to the garden table was overdoing it a bit. It's our last day out here, and you and I have been sitting together for more than six hours, interrupted only, in my case, by some sallies up the flower beds with a large watering can until I heard the ping of the laptop on the table, then I dropped the watering can and rushed back to my neat little terminal. Niels Petter doesn't look at me any more when he walks past; he sends me sidelong glances.

I've already gathered up the extension lead and put it back in the tool shed. The battery is fully charged, but the bowl of cherries is empty.

I'll have to make amends. I've announced that I'll take sole responsibility for a dinner of cod. The boys came back with three large cod this morning. I've hardly looked at them – the fish I mean – but I think I'm the only one who knows about the bottle of Burgundy. Today it will be my little trump card, or perhaps I should say my remission of sins. I hid the bottle in a chest of drawers beneath layers of linen, specifically with the notion of a meal of cod on our last evening.

They always want to go fishing on the last day, and even with natty cool bags I don't like carrying fish back to town. People from Bergen don't zoom about with fresh fish in cool bags. We'd rather go to the market and buy live cod.

But I've thought of something. Could you round off by telling me a bit about what happened at the opening of the new Climate Exhibition?

I'll put on a fish kettle of water, peel some local potatoes, make a salad and lay the table. Then I'll come back and read. It's just that I won't be writing any more myself today.

All right?

☐ You'd left, and for a long time I paced back and forth on the big lawn by the fjord, then I went up to my room and had a shower before going down to the lounge. There I greeted some of the other guests before a mini-seminar about glacier melt, climate and polar research in the Café Mikkel. After a glass of white wine and an amusing intro-duction to the history of the hotel, the village and glacier tourism, we sat down to dinner. I felt rather honoured to be placed at the 'head table'.

After dinner I tried to order a glass of Calvados. I'd been thinking about you the whole time – or about us, I mean, and about that car trip of ours to Normandy. But they didn't have Calvados any more. It was as if I'd dreamt it, as if they'd never had apple brandy in their cellars at any time. Had my memory let me down? But if the thing about the

Calvados was caused by a basic failure of memory on my part, how could I trust anything else I thought I remembered from those days? I stalwartly declined the proffered brandy on the house – I think the young woman had heard on the grapevine that I was giving the lunchtime talk the next day – and ordered a half-litre of beer and a vodka on my own slate.

There were so many animated voices in the hotel lounge that I went up early to my room and turned in. I fell asleep almost at once. I hadn't only had beer and vodka; I'd met you again; I'd been to the shepherd's hut; and I'd been past the birch copse once more.

But I awoke early next morning to the screeching of gulls and went down to breakfast just as they opened the dining-room doors. That morning too I took my coffee out on to the veranda. But you'd left. I sat there alone in the morning sunshine and heard the leaves of the copper beeches whispering in the wind. The gulls mewed and flapped above the Co-op and the old steamship quay. A figure clad in green was fishing from a rowing boat on the fjord.

Something inside me rebelled against this over-idyllic morning atmosphere.

A few hours later we were driven out to the Glacier Museum. We were shown the projected level of the fjord in a few decades' time if we don't deal with climate change.

I found myself wondering if they'd taken account of all that sediment constantly being washed down from the glacier, extending the delta further out into the arm of the fjord. Today they grow potatoes where a thousand years ago the Vikings had a harbour!

When we got to the Climate Exhibition itself we were divided into smaller groups and first entered a small chamber where with roarings and rumblings we could experience the creation of the earth 4.6 billion years ago. The next section we passed through showed us what life on earth was like roughly 40 million years ago, and then how the last Ice Age had affected its surface. Then we went on to a small room where we were shown how the greenhouse effect works and how inhospitable the conditions on our planet would be with no greenhouse effect at all. But then we were told just how disturbing the results of the man-made greenhouse effect were for the original carbon balance, and in the next section we found out what the earth would look like in 2040 and in 2100 if we don't do something drastic now to reduce the emission of greenhouse gasses. It wasn't a very jolly experience. But then, fortunately, we were also shown how it might look here in 2040 and 2100 if we manage to unite the world's inhabitants to take radical measures both against emissions and to halt this disastrous felling of trees and rainforests. It's still possible for this planet to get back on an even keel. In the very last room they were showing some wonderful slides of the earth's many habitats, and more especially of the biological diversity of our planet. David Attenborough was doing the commentary. After stunning pictures of unique plant and animal species he ended by saying, '... but we still have time to act to make changes that will secure the life of this planet. This is the only home we have ...'

After the formal opening we were herded into buses and driven to the Supphellebreen glacier, where an open-air reception had been prepared including mulled wine, strawberries and nibbles. Staff from the hotel had set it all out while we were at the Glacier Museum, and soon the congenial hotel proprietress, who'd clearly been very busy during the previous twenty-four hours, caught sight of me again. I think she'd long been aware that I was there because of the opening of the new Climate Exhibition, and that I'd be giving a short speech during lunch at the hotel a couple of hours later.

She came towards me with a warm, friendly smile, and naturally enquired after you.

'Where's your wife?' she asked.

I just couldn't disappoint her, I just couldn't, Solrun, so I simply said that you'd had to travel home from Fjærland unexpectedly for family reasons back in Bergen.

'Children?' she enquired.

'No, an elderly aunt,' I lied.

She stood there for a second or two hesitating: perhaps she was wondering how personal she could be.

'But have you got children?' she asked.

What was I to say? I was already well into the lie, and I couldn't start into how we'd met out there quite accidentally, not having glimpsed each other for over thirty years. I tried to answer as ambiguously as I could.

'Two,' I said nodding. It wasn't all that far from the truth, what with your two and my two.

But she wouldn't leave it alone: she wanted to know more about our children, and I don't know why, but from then on I stuck to Bergen. I didn't say a word about my girls, but spoke as succinctly as I could about nineteen-year-old Ingrid and sixteen-year-old Jonas – even though it was information I'd only learnt myself a few hours earlier. But like that there was only one lie to maintain, and there's a saying that he who lies must have a good memory. I pretended, in short, to be your husband.

She must have done some rapid mental arithmetic, because she said, 'Really? So it was some years before you had children?'

I thought, So you were hoping to get a confession that we made a baby here at the Hotel Mundal all that time ago when we were youngsters?

But I pointed up at the glacier and said, 'It was much larger back then.'

She nodded and laughed. I didn't know why she

---

laughed. She said, 'It's so good to see you both again!'

Thoughts raced through my head. Perhaps they centred on the separateness of the two entire lives we'd lived. But I also thought about the ferry quay at Revsnes, the police cars at Leikanger and the birch copse up in Mundalsdal.

I nodded in the direction of the glacier again.

'But I'm more worried about the glaciers in the Himalayas,' I said. 'There are several thousand of them which are receding too, and they supply several hundred million people with water.'

I accepted a refill for my glass, turned round to avoid having to answer further questions and walked a few paces down beside the turquoise stream. I strolled on and thought of the book you took up to our room that evening and which you later filched and took back home to Oslo with you. After the encounter with the 'Lingonberry Woman' it became the very sword that separated us. If you hadn't chanced on that book, we might be living together to this day. Well, what do you think?

We could certainly have managed to deal with the 'Lingonberry Woman'. But in the course of a few days you were already fitting her into a very much wider context.

☐ So many thoughts come crowding, Steinn, but now I've got to end. I'm turning the machine off, and I'll contact you from Bergen in the next few days.

———

IV

☐ I'm sitting at my desk in front of the window at Skansen, looking out across Bergen. The weather is gorgeous and already almost autumnal. I've noticed some yellow leaves on the trees for the first time this year, and the days have got shorter.

I'm sitting in what used to be my bedroom when I was a girl. It has belonged to Ingrid since she was three, but when she moved out to share a flat with some other girls a couple of months ago, I got it back. I started on it straight away, pulled up the old wall-to-wall carpeting, polished the floor and painted the walls cream. I've made the room into my own little den again. I call it the library, but Niels Petter treats it as if it were my room, which is generous of him.

Ingrid was so sweet. When she came with a friend to collect the last of her things – she'd left a few boxes of clothes and clothes hangers – she suddenly gave me an ecstatic hug and thanked me for lending her the room. She thanked me for the loan of the room she'd lived in since she was three! But she'd always known it had previously been my room, both when I was a child and when I was grown up.

I've lived in this flat for all but five years of my life.

When I boarded the afternoon express that day I was crying. And what do you think I was doing when we reached Haugastøl? Before we got to Finse, the conductor had sat down next to me and was comforting me. I didn't say a word, and he didn't ask, but he comforted me. After he'd gone out and waved his green flag at Myrdal, he came back. When he found I was still crying, he gave me a cup of tea, not one of those teas in a paper cup you can buy from the trolley, but a proper cup of tea. After that I managed to look up at him and smile. I managed to say thanks. But I couldn't tell him about the Stone Age.

I was going home. I was going home to Mum and Dad. It was the only thing I was completely sure of. I hadn't phoned to tell them I was coming. I couldn't think further than just getting home. They'd just have to take me as I was.

I moved into my old room again. When I met Niels Petter some years later, Mum and Dad had begun to extend Grandma's old house on Ytre Sula, the island in the mouth of the fjord. Dad had begun to 'wind down' as he put it, and finally he sold off the agency. That left him comfortably off. 'It's nice living in Bergen, Solrun,' he mused, 'but I don't think the city is such a wholesome place to *die.'*

They lived out at Kolgrov for more than twenty years, so he was right about that. Dad died quite suddenly three years ago. The story is that he was sitting in his wing chair with a glass of brandy in his hand, a glass that was an old family heirloom, and it fell to the floor and smashed a quarter of a second after he died. And, as I told you, Mum died last winter. I sat with her and held her hand. She only had me.

When I went to Oslo to study, I was exactly the same age as Ingrid is today. It's funny to think about it. That we were so young!

Because it was only a couple of weeks after I arrived in the city that we met. It was after a lecture in the Chateau Neuf building – you wanted a light for your cigarette, perhaps that was just an excuse, but after that we were together all the time. By October we'd moved into the tiny flat in Kringsjå. Sometimes fellow students from the university seemed envious. We were something entirely apart. We were so happy!

Of course I was crying on the train. I cried all the way home to Bergen. I couldn't understand it at all. I knew that suddenly our ideas were completely at odds, but I couldn't see why that should be impossible to live with. After all, we weren't the only couple in the world with different beliefs. Or do you think that a believer and a non-believer can't live under the same roof in a relationship?

How you hated those books, Steinn. And especially one of them. How you despised it, and how you despised me for reading it. Or were you simply jealous? You'd had all my attention for five years. I'd thought about nothing except you and us. After our meeting with the Lingonberry Woman, and after I began reading the book I'd taken home on loan from the hotel, I began to develop a more committed belief in a life to come. Couldn't you simply have let me keep that belief?

Who are you really? I mean today. I asked you what you believe in, and you delivered a long, scientific explanation that was in perfect harmony with the ethos of the faculty where you work. You're clearly no dissenter. Therapsids and *Australopithecus*, etc., etc. Then I asked you again and the only answer I got was everything you *don't* believe in. But I won't give up, Steinn. I'm stubborn, you know. I want to take you right back to where we both began. Before I say more about what I believe in myself, I want to take you back to that enchanted feeling for life we had then, but which neither of us was able to link to even a spark of *hope*. I'm asking, What is the world, Steinn? What is a human being? And what is this cosmic fairy tale we're floating about in like small magical pearls of consciousness? Of psyche, mind and spirit. Can't you discern even a ray of hope for souls like us?

☐ Hello again!

Naturally it was painful to read about your journey home to Bergen.

I also feel I ought to cry touché to the last thing you put your finger on. Maybe I *have* given pedestrian answers to the huge questions you've posed. You'll notice that I've developed a certain amount of tunnel vision over the years, because of all the research and studying. One has to keep to the facts. One can put forward hypotheses and theories, but even they must be founded on something we think we know about.

Perhaps it's the word 'belief' that's deflecting me. It isn't in my vocabulary. I find it easier to speak of *intuition*. I've probably got more intuition than belief especially, perhaps, when we're talking about consciousness.

☐ Write about that then, Steinn. I think intuition is a good word too. For example, you could describe what you dreamt about the night before we ran into each other again. Didn't you say it was a cosmic dream?

☐ That's right, and it's still vivid within me. It's as if I really did experience what took place in the dream. Yes, I really was inside that spaceship . . .

☐ Well, let's hear it.

☐ But the whole day preceding it has been branded on my memory, the day before I met you. I can't quite separate that day from the dream it was to give birth to, even though I did almost nothing but sit on trains and buses and cruise through the landscape. So I really think I ought to begin there.

☐ As far as I'm concerned you can start wherever you like, providing you don't leave out the dream. And you can take all the time you want, because for a number of reasons I can't get back to you before tomorrow evening. For one thing, I just don't feel I can sit here tapping away while Niels Petter's at home. It's not that he can't put up with it, but I can't bear the thought of him sitting there listening to me typing away. I don't like hearing people on keyboards myself. I feel the same sort of distaste as when I'm forced to listen to other people's telephone conversations on buses or trains, for example, or on a footpath in the forest. It just feels depressing and embarrassing. And tomorrow we've got our teachers' planning day. I'm quite looking forward to it. It'll be good to get going again.

☐ That's nice, and it'll suit me too, because I'll need some time. I can't promise when I'll get back to you.

☐ Take all the time you need. I'm here, Steinn.
Now I can hear him clearing his throat, so I'll sign off at once. I think I'll suggest a glass of wine. I'll call it a nightcap, that's part of the family jargon.
He's lit the fire for the first time this year. That'll be cosy.

V

☐ It was Tuesday 17 July 2007. I awoke at the crack of dawn to the sound of a considerable thunderstorm. It was a grey day: leaden clouds hung over Oslo. I was to take the train to Gol and from there the bus to Lærdal and Fjærland, a trip lasting almost nine hours. I've never much liked driving alone, I prefer to go by public transport and be entirely free to sit and read or just relax completely.

Berit drove me to Lysaker station that morning. She had to go to her father's with some clean clothes anyway, and I spent a few minutes on the platform before the Bergen train arrived at 8.21. Here too there were intermittent claps of thunder: it was a really sombre summer morning. There was no rain, but the charcoal-grey clouds gave an almost nocturnal impression, and even though the day was well advanced at that time of year, I saw the lightning each time it rent the sky. Then the Bergen train drew into the station, I found my seat – as always, I'd made certain to reserve a window seat – it was seat number 30 in coach 5.

We were soon in Drammen, and the journey continued

---

northwards up the course of the Drammenselva river towards Vikersund and Hønefoss. The cloud cover was still low, the tops of the trees were generally shrouded in mist, but in the two or three metres beneath the low cloud the visibility was good. The river was in spate, and the trees by the edge of Tyrifjord also had water well up their trunks, and some of the jetties were submerged. That's what it has been like several times this summer, a catastrophic summer many farmers would say, because there has been flood damage in large parts of the country, and especially along the Drammenselva, and much of the harvest has been lost.

I don't know if it was something to do with the weather, but from the very first moment I sat there in deep concentration. Suddenly I felt more than usually alert, a bit cleverer than ever before almost. I felt intensely present in the yellow interior of the carriage as it sped through the mist-settled landscape. And I asked myself, What is consciousness? What are memory and reflection? What is it to 'remember' or 'forget' something? What does it mean to sit here like this and think and think about what it *is* to think? And above all, Is consciousness a cosmic coincidence? Is it pure, simple chance that this universe has, for the moment, a consciousness of itself and its own development? Or is it a fundamental characteristic of the nature of this universe?

*

It wasn't the first time I'd pondered this fundamental and intrinsically obvious question. Occasionally, I've put the same question to biologists and astrophysicists, and their initial reaction has usually been a certain rejection or reticence about the rationale of the very question itself. They seemed almost embarrassed on my behalf. Even asking such questions – as a scientist – is seen by many as being unforgivably naive. If I then repeated the question stressing that I was only asking for an intuitive response, the answer was generally affirmative. Yes, they insisted, consciousness as a phenomenon is no more than cosmic coincidence.

There is no inherent intent, purpose or essence to the universe, and this is generally held to be a self-evident assumption. That life began here, and that the biosphere then developed what you term 'magical pearls of con-sciousness', is nothing more than the result of pure accident. Or as the French biologist and Nobel Prize-winner Jacques Monod expressed it, 'The universe was not teeming with life, nor the biosphere with mankind. Our number simply came up, as fortuitously as at a Monte Carlo gambling table.'

He rejects the category of life as an important or essential cosmic phenomenon in the following words: 'I maintain that the biosphere does not contain a predictable class of objects or phenomena, but constitutes a special event, one that, though certainly consistent with first principles, cannot be inferred from these principles. Therefore on the whole unpredictable.'

This is a useful amplification, and of course one may well take Monod's assertion at face value – although it would seem difficult to point to any example that could verify it. 'Unpredictable' in this context must mean that we are referring to phenomena so singular – and therefore so provincial – that they are very much on the boundaries of physical laws.

But this is not where I stand. Ever since we lived together I've had the intuitive feeling that it most certainly is *characteristic* of the nature of the universe that life and consciousness began here. So perhaps there is a dissenter in me after all, if not as a world citizen, at least as a researcher at the Faculty of Mathematics and Natural Sciences. The majority of the astronomers, physicists and biologists I've met actually insist on the opposite: neither life nor consciousness can be traced back to the primitive, lifeless condition as an 'essential' or 'necessary' product.

The very cognitive paradigm of modern science seems to assume that atoms and subatomic particles – i.e. stars and galaxies – dark matter and black holes, are more essential expressions of the reality of the universe than life and consciousness, which, according to this kind of reductionist science, represent nothing more than purely random, arbitrary and therefore 'unimportant' aspects of nature. The presence of stars and planets is a necessary corollary of the big bang. But the additional presence of life and consciousness is due to nothing more than pure chance, a monstrous accident, a cosmic anomaly.

I was thinking along these lines when the train came into the station at Hønefoss. A message appeared on a small screen above the door at the end of the carriage saying: HØNEFOSS 96 METRES ABOVE SEA LEVEL. Two passengers darted out and lit cigarettes.

It wasn't raining, but a heavy sky hung above the landscape threatening at any moment to burst. Then there was the sound of a whistle, and the train moved on past yellow and green fields on one side and forested hillsides on the other. Dark puffs of cloud drifted over the spruce trees.

I tried to remember how it all began. *I tried to remember the history of the universe.*

Protons and neutrons were created by quarks a few microseconds after the big bang, and slightly later came hydrogen nuclei and helium nuclei. Whole atoms complete with electron shells did not develop until hundreds of thousands of years later, still almost exclusively hydrogen and helium, and these heavier atoms were most probably 'baked' or 'stewed together' in the first generation of stars and thereafter spread out to fertilise the universe. 'Fertilise', yes, and in choosing that word I've been openly tendentious. With the heavier atoms we begin, of course, to draw close to the fount of both life and ourselves, because we are made up of these atoms, as too is the planet on which we live.

There is nothing provincial about 'our' atoms' mass or ability to fuse. The atoms we're made of are found all over the universe. So they must, surely, be said to be essential to the nature of this universe. Particle physics, which has recently enabled us to form an idea of the first minutes of our universe, is also fully capable of explaining precisely why these atoms are necessarily part of the chemical compounds we call molecules.

More complicated, but in cosmic terms far rarer, are the things of which all life is composed and which we call macromolecules. Basic to all living things on our planet are macromolecules such as proteins and the self-reproducing nucleic acids DNA and RNA, which control the formation of proteins and are found in the genetic material of every organism. Common to all life on earth is that it is constructed from carbon compounds and that energy (sunlight) and the presence of flowing water play a crucial part.

There is no longer any great mystery about how the macromolecules of life might have been created on earth upwards of four billion years ago. Many small puzzles remain, but biochemistry has, both theoretically and by means of practical experiment, shown how the building blocks of life could have formed in the oxygen-free atmosphere of our young planet. Only after plant photosynthesis did it acquire an oxygen-rich atmosphere as well as an ozone layer that protected life on the planet from cosmic radiation.

Science, in as far as it feels capable of explaining how life on earth began – for example from a 'primeval soup' of macromolecules – acknowledges at the same time that in such a primeval soup life would *probably* evolve. Everything that happens in nature, happens for a reason. Why shouldn't this also be the case with the creation of life?

Today we know that many of life's building blocks can be manufactured synthetically from simple chemical compounds. The rigid distinction between what used to be called organic and inorganic chemistry simply doesn't exist any longer. The molecules that constitute life have also been discovered in space. And, most recently, organic compounds such as alcohol and formic acid have been shown to exist in interstellar nebulae. Recently too, the amino acid glycine has been demonstrated out in space. These molecules are found in the tails of comets and in distant galaxies billions of light years from the Milky Way. But astrochemistry is a branch of science still very much in its infancy.

Life – or the molecules of life on our planet – may not necessarily have developed here. Both may have come from outer space carried, for example, by a comet. In fact, most of the water on our planet most probably arrived here by comet. Such water wasn't necessarily 'clean', let alone sterile.

I was sitting in reality and summing up the history of the universe. The things that have taken place are remarkable, and it's remarkable how I could sit there acting as the memory of this extraordinary story. Fortunately, I was sitting facing the direction of travel – I usually ask for that when I book – and for a while I looked down over Lake Krøderen on my left. Woolly puffs of cloud hung over the lake like albinoid Zeppelins, but above the white airships was a dark grey sky that was reflected in its waters, making Krøderen as drear and dark as in autumn. No rain fell.

Our own world is, however, the only place in the entire universe where we know for a fact that life exists. Only a few years ago planets outside our own solar system were proved to exist for the first time. The reason this had taken so long was simply that previous technology was incapable of detecting extrasolar planets. In the space of just a few years a couple of hundred planets have been located, and it is now estimated that there are planets orbiting at least a quarter of all the sun-like stars in the Milky Way.

Asked today if they believe that life exists on other planets out in the universe, the majority of astronomers will answer yes. The universe is so incredibly vast that what has happened down here in our own small backyard simply *must* have been replicated in many other places. Or so they will say. The puzzling thing in this context is that many of the same astronomers, without a second thought, are still willing to sign up to Monod's familiar dogma that the universe wasn't 'teeming' with life. But if the universe wasn't teeming with life, then what was its relationship to its most remarkable product?

Whereas a few decades ago we were awash with fanciful ideas about extraterrestrial life, astrobiologists are currently concentrating on the search for water. It becomes more and more apparent as a biochemical hypothesis that wherever flowing water is to be found we may also expect to find life. In fact, it would be more amazing if, having found a fertile little planet one day with nice lakes and flowing water, it did *not* have life, rather than the other way round.

The basic materials are thus universal and can be directly inferred from 'first principles'. Complicated molecules or macromolecules are much rarer. But this is not to say they are any less *universal*.

So ran my thoughts. It was a thoroughly linear but also a distinctly logical chain of thought I was working through.

Perhaps I was the only person on the whole of the planet who was considering his own consciousness or enlightenment that morning. And, who knew, perhaps I was the only one doing so in the entire universe just then. In that case, I was sitting in my yellow railway carriage enjoying a huge privilege.

Just before Nesbyen it began to rain. The blue screen above the connecting door announced in white letters: NESBYEN: PLATFORM ON THE LEFT, 168 METRES ABOVE SEA LEVEL. And after we'd been waved off from the station: WELCOME ABOARD THE TRAIN TO BERGEN. Followed by another cheery message: WELCOME TO THE CAFÉ * EXCELLENT MENU * SNACKS, DINNER * AND CONFECTIONERY.

Between Nesbyen and Gol there was forest on both sides of the train. I sat staring down into the river on my right. I spotted an occasional farm. Now the clouds of mist were right down in the bottom of the valley. It almost looked as if the airy Zeppelins were landing.

There is something in cosmology called the cosmological principle, which states that the universe displays the same characteristics no matter where you go. Provided the scale is large enough, the universe is isotropic, or homogenous and uniform.

Why shouldn't this principle also apply to our question: can we expect to find life spread across the universe in the same way that we find planets, stars and galaxies? Or is the existence of what we term life just something that happened to occur here?

The universe contains something in the order of several hundred billion galaxies, and each one of these has in the region of a hundred billion stars in it. This means we have more than enough chemical factories, to put it mildly. What I mean is, we've had the opportunity to place an incalculable number of chips on that Monte Carlo gaming table! And this demolishes part of the basis for declaring any potential bonanza 'fortuitous'.

It is clearly not fortuitous that a heavy gambler sometimes wins a huge sum. In fact it's typical for him to do so occasionally. When we do bump into people who boast of regular wins on the Lottery or at the races, we sometimes ask just how much these lucky winners bet in total. The question isn't always welcome.

I haven't forgotten consciousness. If we take a glance at our own biosphere, it can't be denied that it was teeming with the nervous systems and sensual apparatus of its organisms. Sight, for example, has developed several dozen times on our own planet without there being any genetic link. And so we can expect that larger organisms on other planets would also have developed a sense of sight of some kind. The reason is obvious: in any biosphere there must be an evolutionary advantage in being able to take in your surroundings, whether it be inhospitable terrain, enemies or prey. Where there is sexual propagation, you must also be able to select a suitable mate. Further senses will also be advantageous in the struggle for survival on other planets, for example hearing, echo location, the ability to feel pain, taste, smell, and maybe some exotic senses we aren't familiar with here.

Every higher organism will require an efficient control centre or 'brain' for coordinating sensual perceptions. Once again, there are examples from our own planet to show how various types of animals have developed nervous systems of a more or less complex and intricate nature, quite independently of one another. It is interesting to note that neurological researchers have studied octopus nerve tissue in order to understand man's own nervous system better.

So, in line with our theory that life is a universally distributed phenomenon, we can say the same about the development of a nervous system and a brain.

Gol, 207 metres above sea level. I gathered my things together, a jacket and a small daysack. The next station is Gol, platform on the right.

Not long after I was standing outside in the fine drizzle. As soon as I'd got a local bus to Gol Bus Station I switched on my GPS and quickly made satellite contact. The time was 11.19 and I was at 60 degrees, 42 minutes, 6 seconds north; 08 degrees, 56 minutes, 31 seconds east; error +/– 20 feet. Sunrise 04.21, sunset 22.38, but it was cloudy and a light rain was falling. Moonrise 08.11, moonset 23.23, but even if it had been a clear summer's day, I'd barely have been able to see the moon in the sky. I was given the following hunting and fishing forecast: AVERAGE DAY. Oh well . . .

At the bus station I sat down with a cup of coffee and a cheese and paprika croissant. But I was still deep in thought, in cosmic thought, and was hardly there at all, even though I permitted myself to be distracted for a few moments by some unusually good eye contact with a woman who was a good deal younger than me. I had the daft notion that she might think I was ten years younger than I really was.

Out in Gol, on the single main road through the town centre, it was now raining cats and dogs. This put me, if possible, in an even more atmospheric frame of mind. I took a small break from my mental enquiries about the fundamentals and wrote down a few key words for the lunchtime talk I was to give a couple of days later. Of course I had no idea that before then you and I would be reunited, even though I hardly need mention that there in Gol I naturally thought back to the time when the two of us had driven through this countryside in a red Volkswagen on our way to the glacier in the west.

———

I'd had a long lunch break, as the bus from Gol didn't leave until 13.20. Not long after we drove into the mist going up Hemsedal. The bus had a display as well. The temperature outside was 14 degrees. Then the mist lifted a little.

As our own planet bears witness, having a brain and a nervous system is a long way from what we call 'consciousness', the more so if by that we mean anything as significant as the actual ability to ponder one's own place in existence, not simply in some habitat but in the universe, not to mention in reality. But then, once vertebrates had raised themselves up on two legs and freed their forelimbs – for the manufacture of tools, for example – there was a decisive advantage in being able to learn some useful tricks, and in having the capacity to share 'survival techniques' with other members of the group, such as descendants. Life with what we call consciousness offered itself as a vacant niche for the human family. If we hadn't occupied it first, sooner or later the representatives of some other order of vertebrates might well have ended up pondering how this universe, including life and consciousness, came into being.

It might be a cheap point, but we should still contemplate the fact that so far 100 per cent of all celestial bodies on which we know for certain that life exists have fostered consciousness, and a consciousness with a potential horizon that stretches almost all the way back to the big bang.

The development of the universe is concerned in no small measure with the formation of ever more differentiated or integrated physical processes. Thus far, the human brain is the most complicated and complex system we know of. It is the consciousness lodged within this organ that continually peers out into the universe, asking on behalf of the entire cosmos, Who are we? Where do we come from?

In semantic terms these terse sentences are so simple and fundamental that it would be no surprise if they were being shouted out into the void from other corners of space too, many light years away from our own galactic backyard. The language might be different in structure, and phonetically its sounds might be hard for us to recognise as language at all, but it could well be that such an extra-terrestrial civilisation would *think* rather like we do, and certainly possess a scientific history not so very different from our own. There too the most prominent of its inhabitants must have fumbled their way down the long and tortuous path towards a greater understanding of the nature of their world, of the birth of the universe and the periodic system of the elements.

The fact that SETI, the Search for Extraterrestrial Intelligence project, spends enormous sums listening out for signs of life – and by definition intelligent life – can hardly be ascribed to a search for something so implausible as another cosmic coincidence a mere few light years away from our own star. It must be because we are looking for corroboration that our own race represents something fundamentally characteristic or essential for the universe as a whole.

But there *are* also arguments for saying that it is only here that there are creatures with universal consciousness. Even if primitive life forms have evolved on other celestial bodies as well, we mustn't forget that from the time life began here it took almost four billion years for the human family to see the light of day, and four billion years is quite an age for a planet. In only one billion years' time the conditions for life will have ceased on our planet, the earth will lose its atmosphere and the water will evaporate.

Perhaps we're alone after all. But for the moment we cannot be completely certain that this universe isn't a geyser of souls and spirits of the most varied physical appearance.

I've just remembered that when I was a child I often used to think about exactly this. Perhaps it's crawling with life out there in the universe, I'd think. It was a stirring thought. But then the exact opposite would strike me. Perhaps life is found *nowhere else* in the entire universe but here. That too was an exciting thought. Both possibilities emphasised the extraordinary miracle of my existence.

---

*

The bus raced on through Hemsedal. I realised, of course, that before long I would pass *the* place. I tried to prepare myself. Perhaps all the thoughts I'd been having about the universe were a part of that preparation. You remember that ferry quay at Revsnes. We had to talk about something so huge that a paltry occurrence on our own planet paled into insignificance against a higher order and an almost infinitely larger context.

The cloud cover was still low, but how can you tell a sea of mist and a layer of cloud apart? The clouds hung only three metres above the ground.

A road sign informed us that Trunk Road 52 across the mountains at Hemsedal was open. Of course it was, it was the middle of summer.

For a long time the road ran up the right side of the river, which was flowing unusually strongly because of the record rainfall just recently, but also because of the late snow-melt in the mountains this summer. We passed a dam – the reservoir was brimful and water was spilling over. So that was the reason the Hemsil had been in spate further down the valley. It fitted in with the water covering the jetties on Tyrifjord – it was all the same watercourse.

Heavily concentrated blobs of seemingly palpable mist bobbed across the floor of the valley. The weather that day had begun to resemble a meteorological joke. Then it thickened up again: only the valley bottom was visible, both mountainsides were shrouded in mist.

I took all this in while focusing at the same time on how incomprehensible it was that I could sit there with definite clear ideas about the universe's history and geography. I was even indulging in various notions of how and why things like me had evolved.

'The universe was not teeming with life, nor the biosphere with mankind. Our number simply came up, as fortuitously as at a Monte Carlo gambling table.'

But it might be tempting to try to play Jacques Monod's reductionist fanfare backwards – just to see how musical or unmusical it would sound: *The universe was teeming with life, and life with the universe's consciousness of itself.*

I didn't think that sounded too bad. It didn't, at all events, run contrary to any intuition I might have, whether that's of any significance or not. This universe is conscious of itself, or it *has* consciousness of itself. Such an obvious but astonishing fact cannot be left entirely to the interpretation of esoteric movements.

For there is something on a higher level, I thought as we approached the watershed, indeed the highest level that can be argued scientifically. Perhaps consciousness 'ought' not to have evolved, and perhaps life 'ought' not to have evolved, as Monod argued. But perhaps the universe 'ought' not to have evolved either.

If, from the first moment onward, our universe had had a minutely different composition, it would have collapsed a few millionths of a second after it came into being. Even microscopic differences in what Monod called 'first principles' would have inevitably led to no universe at all. Just a couple of examples. If, at its conception, the universe hadn't contained just an iota more positive mass than negative mass, the whole thing would have destroyed itself only an instant after the bang. If the huge atomic forces had been just a *little* weaker, the entire universe would have been composed of hydrogen, and if a *little* stronger, there would be no hydrogen here at all. The list is much longer. As Stephen Hawking once put it: 'The odds against a universe like ours emerging out of something like the big bang are enormous.'

The fact that a *viable* universe came about at all is as 'fortuitous' as the emergence of life and consciousness. So Monod's first principles too have arisen just as fortuitously as at a Monte Carlo gambling table. Or, notwithstanding, can we permit ourselves to ponder whether 'something' could have been up there 'behind' or 'beyond' the time and space that was created by the big bang? There is no scientific proof that can entirely preclude a 'something' that may have been 'teeming' with this universe.

———

For a universe to conjure up a consciousness of itself and its own beauty and order, a long list of criteria need to be fulfilled – even *before* the first microseconds after the big bang. This is one such universe. It's a fact we should take note of.

So ran my thoughts. Many professional colleagues would have described them as a kind of heresy. The thinking I was indulging in was certainly well outside the box as far as science was concerned. But this is what I meant by intuition.

The road followed the left bank of the river. For a while we passed through a cultivated landscape, meadows and small copses, before we were back by the river again. Then began the climb towards Bjøberg Mountain Hostel. I noticed a bridge daringly suspended across the river. Our altitude was now around 700 metres. Dense thickets of birch grew on either side of the river.

The mist was even thicker, but I could see all the snow on the mountainside to my left, and some cabins to my right, the last ones, probably, before we were in mountain country proper and building was banned.

We approached Lake Eldrevatnet at the county boundary and the watershed. It was the first time I'd been there since, but I'd steeled myself and was glad I wasn't driving my own car. I didn't look at the lake as we passed it. But I looked at my watch. It was 14.20. I hadn't planned it, but there was a half-bottle of vodka in my daysack. I fished it out discreetly, screwed off the cap and took a long swig. I don't think any of the other passengers noticed. More than thirty years ago, but still so near. She was a mystery. The woman with the shawl, I mean.

Then we were heading down towards the west of the country. The time was 14.29 as we passed the first sharp bend by the precipice. I took another pull at the vodka. It was as if everything I'd been thinking about was linked to what happened back then. We'd tried to get a few hours' sleep out at Revsnes. But we'd just lain there with our eyes closed, talking.

We drove for a while down the fast-flowing river towards Lærdal, but after the medieval stave-church at Borgund the road now went through tunnels. Dense puffs of cloud hovered above the valley floor like weightless lambs, but only here and there. We drove into the centre of Lærdal, where back then we'd decided not to spend the night. Do you remember? We picked up some more passengers and then we dived into the long tunnel out to Fodnes. I was grateful for the new tunnel. I was grateful to avoid another visit to nerve-racking Revsnes.

On the short ferry journey across to Mannheller I did a sort of summing up of what I'd been turning over in my mind almost all the way from Oslo.

*

———

Setting a myriad of details to one side, contemporary science is faced with two gigantic riddles: what actually happened in the universe's first fraction of a microsecond of existence, and the nature of consciousness. Perhaps there is no reason to believe that any connection exists between these two uniquely great mysteries of man and science. But a connection can't be ruled out either. If I were asked to place a bet, I would say there *was* such a connection.

I believe there must be a deeper explanation – or *root* and *cause* – behind the physical laws that have shaped our universe. And there you have my essential credo. If there is something 'divine', it must be behind the big bang. After that, it's my opinion that natural laws, and natural laws only, have held sway, and that absolutely all that happens has natural causes.

If you want to search for 'divine proofs', the most obvious places to seek them would be in the cosmic constants, or in what the atheist Jacques Monod called 'first principles'. Because, as I've said, the only things I don't believe in are 'revelations' of supernatural forces.

My chain of thought had come to an end, and soon I'd be at the end of my bus trip across the country. The only thing I'll add is that I think you'd have to search a long time before you found a physicist who was willing to go as far as I've done in pointing out that life and consciousness really could be essential characteristics of our universe. And I haven't based my reasoning on any revelation or faith; it springs straight out of my reading of nature itself.

A new tunnel at Mannheller, but soon we were looking down at Kaupanger on our left, where once the two of us had disembarked from the ferry, then up into a new sea of fog, before we drove through Sogndal and on over another mountain crossing.

When we emerged from the long tunnel high up on the mountainside above Fjærlandsfjord, I could see nothing but mist below, but even though I'd never been on this road before, I knew quite well that the old landscape lay waiting for me under the mist. Then we bowled into another tunnel, and when we emerged from that one I found myself beneath the cloud cover and could see Supphelledal, Bøyadal and Mundalsdal.

But then the thought struck me: Is she there? Is she coming too? It was pure reflex. I knew how irrational the impulse was.

I got off the bus at the Glacier Museum, rang the hotel and a car picked me up a few minutes later. Soon I was back in the old timber building, after more than thirty years. Room 235 had a good view down to the fjord, the store and the bookshops, but also up to the glacier and moun-tains. For the mist had again turned into isolated puffs that hovered low over the fjord, and from my hotel window I could see above them.

The dining room was full of people. It was good to see the old place flourishing, but perhaps some of it was due to the opening of the new Climate Exhibition. I ordered a 25-cl carafe of the house red at ninety kroner. I couldn't work out the variety of grape or the country of origin, but it was good wine, perhaps Cabernet Sauvignon. I was served a four-course dinner: west-coast salad, cauliflower soup, fillet of veal and strawberries and cream.

After dinner I went up to my room and unpacked. I took a swig of vodka and gazed out into the summer night. It was raining heavily, pouring down. The gulls were screaming above the fjord and from the roof of the Co-op. I took another nip from the bottle before turning in.

And then I met you on the veranda next morning. You'd both arrived immediately after dinner, while I was up in my room with the vodka bottle. I thought of us, naturally. But you were already there at the hotel. You'd been given a more basic meal in the café long after the coffee trolley had been wheeled out of the service area and the dining room was empty of diners.

I lay awake for a long time listening to the gulls crying. As I rested my head on the pillow and closed my eyes

I thought, Inside here. It's so lovely and warm *being* inside here. It's so good and warm being me.

Then I was swept up by my amazing dream. It felt as if it lasted all through the night, well, much longer than that, and even now it feels like something I really did experience.

I *did* experience it.

And there I'll leave my small odyssey. I've sat writing all day long, almost without stopping to eat. I've had coffees and teas, and a couple of times I've been down to the corner cupboard and taken a couple of nips.

And you? Are you back home after your planning day?

□ Yes, I'm back, but I think you ought to be able to keep away from that corner cupboard. It's hardly five o'clock. Couldn't you simply have a rule about not opening that cupboard before eight or nine in the evening? But we've talked about this before. I used to pop into the Grill early in the evening to see what you were doing. And you'd already be sitting there with a beer!

□ There, you see, even then I was wrestling with colossal thoughts. Don't you get just a tiny bit giddy too at the thought that you are *a part of this universe*? I wrote that I could glimpse a correlation between my own consciousness and the big bang 13.7 billion years ago. And instead you start talking about a couple of measures from some rotten little corner cupboard in Kongleveien. In a way it's moving that you're still capable of feeling such ... concern for me.

☐ I know. Perhaps it is moving.

☐ But give me your answer. What do you think of my musings as I travelled across the country from Lysaker to Fjærland?

☐ I don't really know what to say ... I'd have to say roughly what your young female student would: That's interesting, Steinn! And this time I'm not being sarcastic, I really mean it. It's also a delight for me to read sentences you've written like: 'But for the moment we cannot be completely certain that this universe isn't a geyser of souls and spirits of the most varied physical appearance.' And this isn't bad either: 'I believe there must be a deeper explanation – or *root* and *cause* – behind the physical laws that have shaped our universe.' Perhaps these words do contain what you call an essential credo, and so you've at least tried to answer the question I asked, about what you *believe*.

But I did ask for something more besides. I wanted to hear your dream. But yet again I got a materialistic thesis. I don't doubt for a second that it's a tour de force as science, or even as a piece of travel writing, but you only talk about the outer shell around our spiritual nature. To me it's like dwelling more on the oyster shell than on the well-nourished pearl within. There are several thousand empty oysters for every one containing a pearl.

You never cease to amaze me!

□   I'm sitting in a space capsule orbiting the earth. I feel weightless. It feels as if I have no body. I am pure consciousness.

The earth beneath me is covered in dust and soot. The whole planet is black. I see no oceans, and I see no land. Even the Himalayas can't pierce the dark atomic winter with a nunatak. I shout, Houston! Houston! But I know it's no use. The radio is dead. The asteroid I was meant to head off has presumably exterminated the whole of mankind, and perhaps all the vertebrates, at least those that lived on land.

I continue orbiting the charred planet reliving what has happened. Once again an asteroid strike has expunged almost all life, just as it did between the Cretaceous and Tertiary periods, or between the Permian and Triassic periods. The last time it eliminated all the dinosaurs. This time there may not even be a single mammal left. And it's my fault! Only I can be blamed for what's happened.

———

*

The huge asteroid, many kilometres in diameter, had been on a collision course with the earth for a long time. The United Nations had set up a Crisis Committee, and for the first time in history every nation had co-operated to save the planet from destruction.

Meticulous plans had been laid to send up a manned spaceship carrying a large atomic warhead. It was to be a suicide mission. I'd volunteered to go, together with Hassan and Jeff. The bomb would be detonated as we neared the asteroid, but far enough away to prevent it being blown into small fragments. We were simply to nudge the asteroid off course, so that it would miss the earth by a good margin.

At the final briefing before we blasted off there was a 99 per cent chance that the asteroid would hit the earth. Of course, we didn't need to do anything ourselves to detonate the bomb. The computers looked after all of that. Our job was simply to keep a steady course for the hostile object, and the bomb would be triggered at precisely the right distance. The mission was easy.

We were three amongst many hundreds of willing astronauts. There had been a long programme of physical and psychological tests, but the final choice had been made by lottery. This ensured that each and every one of the people selected would still have a fair chance of escaping. It had all been voluntary, only the very last round was like Russian roulette. But as soon as we three were chosen – the winners or the losers, depending which way you looked at it – we became heroes. We were the ones who were going into space to save the planet from annihilation. We were pioneers. We'd been so proud to be selected.

We were to make for the asteroid between Mars and Jupiter. The whole of mankind, and perhaps the entire biosphere, was dependent on us, on our precision and composure.

I was the one who failed. Suddenly I panicked. There were a few minutes left before we were to die. The final message over the radio was, 'Well, good luck, boys! Have a drink now. And *thanks*!'

But I didn't want to die. I wanted to live a bit longer, and at the critical moment I'd steered the craft a few degrees off course and made the mission impossible to accomplish. I remember how Hassan and Jeff remonstrated, but it was too late. I hadn't been trained well enough. Or tested well enough.

In the light from the sun we saw the asteroid shoot past us. According to the last prognosis it was certain to strike the earth, and once that happened there was a 99 per cent chance that all humanity would be wiped out.

*

The asteroid was vast. It had a lewd shape. It was reminiscent of a picture by Magritte. It would hit Central Asia, but the point of impact was totally immaterial; collision with the earth would be fatal for the whole planet.

I'm cruising around a charred planet, but I can't make out the continents. Soot and dust are rising high into the atmosphere, it's an atmosphere that has obviously been seriously damaged. I think back to what had occurred in the capsule.

I remember now that I'd felt ashamed. Hassan and Jeff sat and stared. Jeff raised the palms of his hands the way you do when everything has gone wrong, and leant back in resignation, but Hassan began to cry. I sensed scorn from Jeff and an infinite grief from Hassan. Hassan was a practising Muslim and was certain that he'd go straight to heaven if his mission was successful. I'd found this certainty hard to understand because he was equally convinced that God would decide if he succeeded or not. So surely God had already enacted his will. But I couldn't take all this shame any more. With a few deft manoeuvres I managed to cut them both off from the oxygen supply. This meant that I'd extended my own life in the capsule. I'd now got three times longer to live than I'd had a few minutes previously. I steered the ship back towards earth.

————

I had to see what had happened to my planet. Things couldn't have been worse, that much was obvious. I had enough fuel to get the spaceship circling the black planet, and sufficient oxygen for quite a number of orbits.

I want to employ the last hours I have left in thinking carefully about what it all meant. It's a time for reflection. What was life? What *was* consciousness? For just now I'm completely certain that reason and intellect haven't evolved in any other part of the universe except on the scorched planet I'm circling at the moment. I am the universe's sole remaining consciousness of itself.

Suddenly I feel such a hopeless sadness on behalf of the entire cosmos at the thought that now this universe will move into such a stunted phase. A universe with consciousness and one without are two thoroughly different things. But I'm sad on my own account too. I have so little time left to be me. If I hadn't managed to steal Jeff and Hassan's time, all three of us would have been dead by now, and the consciousness of the universe would already have expired completely. It feels important that I've extended the universe's consciousness of itself.

Then I start to think back on my own life. Or, rather, I don't think, I simply am back there in the 70s and can see you up in Kringsjå: you're so light-hearted, smiling mischievously, and we're doing all the things we used to do. We cook dinner and walk to the café in the forest at Ullevålseter, we cycle to the university and sit at opposite ends of the sofa revising. We tour Normandy by car and go out to the small island we can walk to at low tide – you pick up a blue starfish from the seabed! – and we go on a cycling trip to Stockholm. We mess about in the old dinghy we borrowed from an elderly farmer at Toten. He realised we were mad. That was the only reason he lent it to us. The man had sympathy with us because he knew we were mentally deranged.

I look down on a seared planet. It is my own cradle, the cradle of consciousness. At the same time I can choose to *be* down there, whenever or wherever, during the time I lived on earth, like that roadside in Sweden where we had to stop because my bicycle had a puncture. I got so cross, but you rebuked me, and now, from high up here in my orbit, after your destruction and that of the entire world, I realise you were right that morning. You can't get into a mood just because you have to patch an inner tube, you said. It's summer, silly. And we're alive!

I'm down there now and rediscovering it all. We've borrowed your parents' car and are driving from Bergen to Rutledal. We stand on the deck of the ferry and look out across Sognfjord, then we put in to Krakhella in the narrow sound between Losna and Sula. We drive across the islands and take the little ferry to Nåra. The sculptured archipelago is like a world apart with all its inlets and headlands, channels and lakes. We drive the final kilometres out to Kolgrov, but first you want me to park the car at a particular spot to show me the best view across the sea. You're transported with joy at having me in your childhood paradise, you're quite giddy. We pull up in front of your grandmother's house, and when I meet Randi, I feel I've known her forever, but that's just because I can see so much of you in her. We're like kids out there. We go to Eide's Groceries and buy sweets and ice creams. In the evenings we lie on our beds in the blue room whispering about what we've seen and explored throughout the long summer day.

It all revolves around two stories, my own history and the history of the universe, but the two histories blend, for I wouldn't have had a history if the universe hadn't had its history, and I've also spent half my life studying that history, and if it wasn't for me, the universe would have no consciousness of its own merits. There is no longer any other memory but mine.

I sit for long periods in my capsule watching the history of the planet and the universe pass in review before me like some cosmic cavalcade, before the era of memory and consciousness irrevocably ends in a few hours' time; and when I think this way, on behalf of such a huge amount more than myself, I'm sitting in the capsule the entire time, as if that's where I'm located and *exist* when these thoughts are thought. Never once do I experience a time of partial wakefulness, as one often does in dreams, when I know I'm dreaming but, completely unconcerned, continue to dream on. I *am* in that spaceship after a huge asteroid has struck the planet below me. I remember the details of the instrument panel, all the screens and displays, and I can see Jeff and Hassan so clearly – I know them so well, better than anyone else, the features and lines of each of their faces, we've spent so many hours together in that cramped capsule, and now they're lying lifeless in their seats.

But there's a duality in the way I experience all this, for at the same time I'm able to move out of the spaceship and be together with you in all these places we visited, it's as if I'm having some powerful out-of-body experience. The whole thing is totally disjointed and illogical, but to some extent I'm able to choose where I want to be down there, and when, like the spiritual journeys of a shaman. When we're together in Normandy, we're really there. When we're each sitting on a boulder eating grilled trout on the Hardangervidda plateau, we're really doing it, because I can even evoke the smell of the cooked fish. There is no life in between, no chronological time, just a continuum, an eternity, like an enormous dish from which small pieces of mosaic can be plucked – no, the pieces of mosaic are made of coloured glass and are held in a kaleidoscope into which I gaze as I sit in my spaceship, and I can choose which piece of memory I want to focus on and relive.

Suddenly I get the idea that you're still alive down there under the thick carpet of soot and dust and charcoal. It strikes me that perhaps you're the only person that has survived. This is dream logic or, more accurately, dream's total lack of logic. I get the notion that you've got to help me down. You've survived because you'd sought shelter in one of the deep tunnels in the west of the country. Only you can get me down. Soon I'll fall into the arm of a fjord below the Jostedalsbreen glacier, and you'll be the one who opens the capsule bobbing in the middle of the fjord. In the dream it seems so easy, because you can just row out in a boat and collect me.

I relive the rowing trip we took across the fjord that time. We lay down in the grass by the old hay barn on the far shore and sunbathed. You felt you couldn't sunbathe topless on the lawn in front of the hotel. We're lying out there now. It's hot, at least twenty degrees, but we've left a bottle of fizzy drink to cool at the water's edge. A bit later we row back, and we catch sight of a couple of porpoises swimming into the fjord from Balestrand. They circle the boat several times, and we become alarmed, but soon they swim out again.

*

I go round and round the black planet. It's so unutterably painful that there are only a few hours left until the universe is bereft of spiritual life. I clasp my hands and pray to a God I don't believe in: *Please, please turn the clock back! Please let me have one more chance! Can't the whole world have just one more chance?*

Then something strange happens, it wouldn't have worked in a film, but this is quite a different genre, this is a dream. Jeff and Hassan suddenly begin to stir and open their eyes. And then? Then all the dust and soot around the planet dissolves, and I see the dark blue Atlantic below me. Now we're flying high up towards the west coast of Africa ...

It was then I awoke. I couldn't believe it had been a dream. The strangest thing of all was Jeff and Hassan. They'd been so vivid and real, and they were so unlike anyone I'd met in real life. The bewitching realisation that parallel realities must exist and that such spiritual journeys really are possible stayed with me.

Outside, shreds of mist were still floating over the mountainsides. But there was good visibility to the fjord.

I went down and had breakfast, totally immersed in my dream. Then I took an over-full cup of coffee out on to the veranda.

And there you were!!!

VI

□ Yes, there I was. And then, perhaps, you realised you'd had a prophetic dream?

□ Well—

□ Are you doing anything special?

□ No. Why?

□ I'm wondering if you're busy this evening.

□ On the contrary. Berit just went off to the theatre with her sister.

□ In that case I think we should continue our dialogue. Niels Petter is out playing bridge with some friends. We've got the whole evening to ourselves. It's so nice to sit here and look out across the city. But I feel restless . . .

And you? Where are you at the moment?

☐ I'm at home in a small study on the first floor. My desk too is in front of a window which looks out over the town. Darkness has just begun to descend on Oslo, and the city lights have got brighter. I can see the lights of Ekeberg and Nesodden.

☐ I'm looking down on the harbour and the church of Korskirken – and Johanneskirken, which is right in the background. Then I can see the fire station and the City Hall just in front of the Lille Lungegårdsvann pond.

But there I was, you wrote, and perhaps then you realised your dream had been precognitive . . .

☐ But when I arrived at the old hotel the previous evening, it felt as if I could bump into you at any moment, in the lounge or the dining room. Each stair up to my room reminded me of you, every picture and woven wall hanging. And the old telephone kiosk, do you remember that? Or, to put it quite differently, what I noticed most forcibly when I arrived at the Hotel Mundal was that you weren't there. Everywhere you were – absent. And so it's hardly surprising that I dreamt of the time we used to live together. The uncanny thing was that you were suddenly standing there on the veranda. That was what I described as an extraordinary fluke. But the fact you were there wasn't the *cause* of my dreaming about you.

☐ No? All night long, while you were orbiting your charred planet, I was lying in a bed nearby and sleeping as well. Don't you think, considering all the things you dreamt, that it's distinctly probable that some sort of mental osmosis occurred between us? Did you know that you're more susceptible to telepathy and foresight when you're dreaming, and in what is called REM-sleep? The phenomenon is officially called *paranormal dreams*. There's been a certain amount of laboratory research into it, but there is also anthropological material that shows exactly the same thing. Have you read the Icelandic saga of Gunnlaug Ormstunge? Better known are Joseph's dreams in Genesis. All these were typically clairvoyant or precognitive dreams.

☐ My mother read the saga of Helga, Gunnlaug and Hrafn to me when I was young. You haven't forgotten that I was born in Iceland? The question is, just how true such saga dreams literally are. But I do agree that interpreting dreams is almost universal, I mean with regard to expressing something about the future.

☐ Your dream certainly had all the characteristic hallmarks of what I would call a *lucid* dream. It was a typical revelatory dream. Wouldn't you agree that it was extraordinarily intense and expressive?

☐ I agree about that. I told you even when we were up at

the shepherd's hut that I'd had an uncommonly vivid and forceful dream, and that it was odd to be walking with you only a few hours after I'd woken up. Or should I say only a few hours after you got me down from space? As far as I was concerned, the dream said a lot about how those years we'd shared continue to live inside me and affect me; and perhaps I also have a feeling that since then I've been a little in 'orbit', that the life I've lived subsequently has been rather on the outside. Most dreams are probably also fostered by something that happened to you the day before. I'd been travelling through a mist-shrouded landscape.

☐ But at the same time it was a terrifying and nightmarish dream. It's as if you're thirsting for something to believe in. The notion of being the universe's sole consciousness is begging to be refuted. I mean that you're begging yourself to repudiate this misconception. And there are more of us, Steinn. More souls in the universe, I mean. I believe we're a myriad of spirits. I don't know how many of course, but I think we're almost infinitely many, infinite as the glints of sun on the sea on a summer's day.

☐ Sorry, Solrun. I just can't follow you in that sort of thing. Will you forgive me?

☐ I more than forgive. I'm wholeheartedly indulgent. You obviously believe that matter will outlive the spirit, that was also apparent from your dream. This entire, monstrous universe will one day survive us like so much external junk. I believe the exact opposite. Our souls will almost certainly outlast all this material sludge. Because if there's one thing we agree on, it's that all natural things will eventually decay.

☐ Yes, unfortunately. It's an inescapable consequence of the second law of thermodynamics.

☐ But there's no equivalent principle that says that the ravages of time can make even the slightest dent in what is spiritual.

☐ Because we have a free soul that survives the death of the body. I think I know what you mean.

☐ Imagine that you're going for a walk in the woods. You take a path you haven't been on for some weeks, and suddenly you come to a brand new log cabin you've never seen before. It's peculiar enough that a cabin's been erected there anyway but, while you're standing there looking, the door opens and out comes a smiling man with bright blue eyes and sparkling white teeth. He seems almost made-to-measure. He bows deeply. Good morning, good morning! he calls. The setting is surreal, mysterious.
Then the question. What has happened? Was it the

cabin that first assembled itself out of some trees in the wood and then created the man to animate it? Or was it the other way round: did the man build the cabin and then move in?

I'm asking what you think most plausible, whether what came first was something spiritual or something material. In your description about your journey you summed up by saying that you could glimpse a connection between consciousness and what happened 'in the universe's first fraction of a microsecond'. Now I'm asking you which you think came first: consciousness or the enormous discharge of energy that occurred during that first second.

Didn't you in fact argue that 'something could have been up there behind or beyond the time and space that was created by the big bang'? They're your words. And so isn't it misrepresentation to describe the big bang as the *beginning* of everything? What we know as the world's greatest mystery may have been nothing more than rigid continuity from one state to another.

☐ I don't know. No, I really don't know any more. We know nothing.

☐ In your dream you were in despair. You felt a great need to be saved from your materialistic view of the world.

You even went so far as to pray to a God you didn't believe in. Surely that's real helplessness.

But don't you see any possible meeting of minds? Not even after a dream like *that*? It was like one great, lucid announcement that you actually possess a very intense spiritual life. And your prayer was answered. That must mean that, at least subconsciously, you doubt your own atheism.

Haven't you ever had any *experiences*, Steinn? Have you never been through anything you might interpret as a hint of something spiritual or transcendental?

It's only just ten o'clock, and I'm not going to bed for a long time yet.

☐ Yes, I have experienced something – it happened back in the 1970s. I'd meant to tell you about it that day in July, when we sat down on the ruins of the old shepherd's hut, it was just that I wanted to get that powerful dream out of my system. Then the heifers appeared, and you know why we didn't get so much talking done on the way down. It's almost painful to admit at our age, I think we said as much, but there was something, you know, that suddenly made us a little embarrassed with one another. All at once there was nothing more to say. That's why I suggested that we could at least start sending each other the odd email. You remember I mentioned that when we were down at the rifle range and the red barn. And as soon as we found your husband in the bookshop, all conversation between us was at an end. I'd thought that the three of us could round off by having a coffee together, but it wasn't to be.

It was a year after you'd left me that I heard from you again. You asked me to pack up your things and send them to Bergen. It was no easy task, as you hinted in your recent email, because most of what we owned, we'd bought together. We'd lived in the same flat since we were nineteen, so it wasn't easy, five years later, to draw a line between yours and mine. But I think I was open-handed enough and you weren't done out of anything. Sentimental value was an important initial consideration, and I knew the things you were fondest of, though of course there's no law that says that what one person treasures most will necessarily be less valued by the other; often it's quite the opposite. You remember the glass bell we bought in Småland after we'd been to Skåne. I was fond of that too, but I wrapped it carefully in tissue paper and sent it to you. I hope it survived the journey and that it's still in one piece.

I once heard a story about a couple who wanted to leave each other. They both agreed it was the best thing to do, and in the spirit of co-operation they began to divide up all their books. But it soon became apparent that any book one of them wanted to keep was also much coveted by the other. This state of affairs repeated itself the more books they tried to divide, and then they began to talk about some of these works, and it dawned on them that they were far too alike to part. They're still together today, and they regard the cause of their planned separation as a totally insignificant episode.

In our case books played a large part as well but with the opposite effect. I'm thinking of that library of yours, but I particularly have one book in mind, and you know which one that is. Sometimes there's more destructive power in one book than in a mere 'episode'.

Once I'd packed up your things and sent them off, I felt that our separation was sealed. We needed no documents when we lived together, and none now that we'd parted.

But when I'd been to the post office and sent the three boxes that morning, I didn't return home. I took the Volkswagen and drove out on to the ring road and on down Drammensveien, just as we might have done, because I wasn't sure where I was heading until I'd passed Sandvika on my way to Sollihøgda and Hønefoss.

Five hours later I passed Haugastøl. I drove a bit further south and up on to the Hardangervidda plateau, parked the car and found my way back to our old camp. I mooched around up there and sat down for a good long while before returning to the car and driving off.

*

The place itself looked as if we'd only left it the day before. I crawled into the 'cave' itself and found our couch in there, as well as the uncured lamb's fleece. You thought that if anyone found the skin while rounding up sheep, the farmer might get compensation. You always wanted to pay your debts. But the fleece lay there undisturbed.

I can't say that smoke was still rising from the hearth, but the charred remains of juniper and dwarf birch lay between the stones just as we'd left them. I found lots of other traces of us too. I began, more or less systematically, to engage in some erotic archaeology. You'd left one of your green gloves behind, a five-kroner piece and a hairclip of light metal, but wasn't the hairclip rather a breach of the rules for the Stone Age? I can't remember you using it. Perhaps it just fell out of your pocket. Our hair got pretty unruly after a while. Soap and shampoo were definitely out; we used dwarf birch, lichen and moss instead of soap. I turned up a couple of our home-made fish hooks, and I almost felt a prick of shame at the many fish bones strewn about outside our cave, but I'm sure they did that at the famous Cro-Magnon cave too. I think we told each other as much. We're allowed to be a bit messy, we said. For us it was important to live as authentically as possible. We were human beings, but only just. We'd only just crossed the threshold from being animals, so we couldn't be too refined, we had to be a bit rough and ready.

*

Then all at once – for it did happen suddenly – it was as if I'd lost my grip on myself and had melted into the landscape around me. The fact that it happened there and then felt coincidental, because I'd done nothing to bring it about. I was simply suffused with the feeling that what I'd thought of as 'me' and 'mine' was no longer valid; it had been nothing but an illusion.

I surrendered myself, and it didn't feel like any loss, it only felt liberating and enriching, because simultaneously the idea washed over me that I was far more than that miserable ego I'd been so worried about before. I wasn't just me. It was as simple as that. I was the entire plateau around me too, the whole country, in fact everything that existed, from the tiniest little aphid to the galaxies up above. Everything was me, and I *was* all this.

It was an indescribable state of consciousness I found myself in. I both felt and knew that I *was* the boulder I was sitting on – and that one over there, and that, and that, as well as all the heather, crowberries and dwarf birch that clothed me. Then I heard the melancholy call of a golden plover, but that was me as well: it was I who called, and it was my own attention I was calling.

I smiled. Beneath a ruffled surface of sensual impressions, of will and desire, I'd always had a deeper identity, something still and quiet which was related to everything in existence, and now, in the moment it became apparent to me, my disturbed surface had become calm. I'd been the victim of the world's biggest bluff, that 'I' was supposed to be something entirely divorced from everything else. But I certainly wasn't experiencing anything transcendental. On the contrary, it was radically of this world.

I had a strong feeling of timelessness. I can't say I felt as if I'd been detached from time, but rather that I felt woven into it, and not just spliced into the present fleeting moment but into all time. I wasn't just living my own life, I wasn't just the there and the then, I was before and now and afterwards. I was growing in all directions, and I would always do so, for all was one, and one and all was me.

Then it all began to wear off, the experience I'm describing was a passing one. I'd had a happy glimpse of eternity, of everything that existed before or would exist after me, even though the state itself only lasted a few seconds. But with my out-of-body experience I'd gained an entirely new insight, a dimension I knew I'd carry with me all my life.

So much for the experience or state of consciousness itself. Although what I've been trying to recall was genuine enough, I believe with hindsight that it's also possible to some degree to arrive at the same perception through pure thought.

We often say that we're *of* the world, *in* the universe or *on* the planet. Fine. But mightn't it be a tempting game, not to mention a liberating exercise, to drop these troublesome prepositions? I *am* the world. I *am* this universe.

———

I arrived at an almost inexpressible state of consciousness up there on the plateau. But what I experienced was *true*. See, it's actually true – I am the world.

Well, what's your opinion? Can you glimpse any hope of reconciliation along the lines I've sketched out here? Are you capable of enjoying the thought that there'll be hares, grouse and reindeer dashing across the Hardangervidda plateau in a hundred, a thousand or a million years' time? And can you at the same time feel that in some way you *are* that profusion that will abound after you? Can such a consciousness also give you an iota of peace of mind, as much perhaps as the ethereal notion of your own little 'I' outliving its earthly existence to become 'spirit' in a paradise of the soul?

Imagine the following dilemma. On the table in front of you there are two buttons you can press. If you press one of them, you'll die immediately, and there'll be no individual life after this one, but at the same time you'll ensure that both mankind and every other life form on this planet will continue for aeons to come. For countless generations little girls will run about the rocky seashore just as you once did in the late 50s. I can see them in my mind's eye, you know. I sense there are swarms of people around that next corner. But there's another button on the table in front of you, and if you press that one instead, you will live hale and hearty until you're over a hundred. However, and this is the dilemma, the whole of humanity and all life on earth will die at the same time as you.

Which one would you choose?

I believe that I wouldn't hesitate to choose the first. I'm not trying to claim any kind of piousness or altruism. But I am not simply me, and I don't simply live my own life. If I look deeper, I'm also mankind, and hopefully *that* will thrive after I'm gone as well; I actually have an egotistical desire that it should, for much of what I think of as me is anchored in something outside my own body. On that point we're in some agreement. I'm not just this body of mine. Not everything rides or falls with it.

Nowadays we're constantly fooled into believing that our own ego is the very centre of the universe. But isn't that a very exhausting way to live? I mean with the view that the hub of the universe only has a few years or decades left to exist.

I experienced a liberation of spirit up there on the plateau. I felt as if I'd been delivered from the slavery of egocentricity. It was as if some constraining bands had burst, the bands of the ego or the self.

But there's more to tell.

Although the time was about four o'clock when I returned to the car, I felt I ought to carry on just a bit further west instead of turning home for Oslo immediately. Soon I'd crossed Hardangervidda, and felt I might as well drive down Måbødal too, then I took a ferry across the fjord from Kinsarvik and drove on to Nordheimsund and then all the way to Arna, via Kvamskogen. Once there I considered turning round, because evening had arrived, and it was more than 400 kilometres back to Kringsjå.

But I couldn't go back now that I was so close to you, so I just drove into Bergen and parked the red Volkswagen at Nordnes. Then I began to wander the streets. It seemed absurd, I realised that even as I crossed Hardangerfjord: I might just as well have delivered your parcels by car instead of sending them by post. The whole thing was stupid, because if I'd had the parcels, I'd have had a proper excuse to look you up.

But I was sure that I'd meet you in the street soon, after driving so far. I turned one corner, and when you weren't there I felt convinced that I'd bump into you around the next one. Finally, I made my way up to Skansen and paced up and down there for a while. I'd been to your parents' flat in Søndre Blekeveien a couple of times before, but I couldn't just stand outside the house, it would have been too melodramatic, and I felt I couldn't simply ring at the door. I was frightened of getting your parents mixed up in things.

You'd surely take an evening walk soon, I thought, you who'd always been so finely attuned to where I was and when I'd turn up. You'd use your sixth sense and come out to meet me. But you *didn't have* a sixth sense, Solrun, at least not that evening. Not if you were at home anyway, for all I knew you might be in Rome or Paris. It started to rain. I hadn't the money for a hotel, so I walked back to Nordnes still with the feeling that I'd run into you before I reached the car. But I had to climb into the red Volkswagen wet, dishevelled and alone. I had to put the key in the ignition and start the engine, but the battle still wasn't lost, because I went on searching for you as I drove out of the city, wondering if you might be on your way home after visiting a friend. Even at Nordheimsund I caught sight of a figure that bore a passing resemblance to you. But no. I managed to get across the fjord and was back home in Kringsjå next morning. I just shut myself in and cried. I drank and slept.

The severance between us was surgical, and there was no anaesthetic.

☐ Well, Steinn . . .

After writing that letter to you I nursed a small but passionate hope that instead of posting me my things, you'd put them in the car and drive across the mountains with them. It was the very *last* chance we had. Naturally I thought about you a lot in the days that followed, and one evening I got the idea that you were walking un-happily round the streets of Bergen. I had the notion that you'd got my stuff in the red Volkswagen, but that you hadn't the courage to come here and hand it over personally. So I went outside. It had begun to rain, and I dashed in again for an umbrella, but I also had the feeling that I must find you quickly. I went down to the Fish Market and up to Torgallmenningen, and then on to Engen, and I visited Nøstet and Nordnes as well. But you weren't anywhere. After that I wasn't so sure you'd been in Bergen at all, but I did at least feel certain that you'd been thinking hard about me that evening, and I knew that we were still fond of each other.

But then the years started to pass. I seem to remember that for form's sake I sent you a few lines telling you I'd moved in with Niels Petter, and a bit later I heard rumours from Oslo that you'd met Berit. Strangely enough, I wasn't pleased at the news. I was jealous ...

For me, the strangest thing you said was that you'd been up to our cave again. I'm certain I never used any hairclips; it must have fallen out of one of my anorak pockets, and the five-kroner piece might as easily have been yours.

But did you find any cigarette butts? Don't you remember? Of course we weren't supposed to have *cigarettes* in the Stone Age. So we had to stop smoking too, or at least resist the temptation while we were up there. But one day you came back from a fishing expedition and I could smell quite distinctly that you'd been smoking, because you couldn't get out of giving me a kiss. You admitted it at once and were terribly guilty. You were so upset, Steinn. You gave me the packet at once, and it went up in flames on the campfire that evening.

☐ But what's your impression of the experience I had on the plateau?

☐ Yes, I know, I think I understand what you were describing, and perhaps what you experienced wasn't necessarily so incompatible with what I believe myself. In material terms all is obviously one – with solid roots back to your big bang. But aren't we first and foremost matchless individuals? Aren't we unique people? *That* was what we used to say. Today I would add that we're spiritual beings.

Of course it's funny to think that the atoms and molecules that my body leaves behind it can later become part of a hare or a mountain fox. But for me it's an amusing thought and nothing more. Because I'd be dead, Steinn! Don't you see? That was what I couldn't bear the thought of in the old days. That I'd only be me for a short while more. I wanted to last! And today I have a more miraculous hope than you, a more miraculous belief.

I'm not going to try to belittle the importance of the beautiful experience you had on the plateau the year after I'd gone. But I doubt how reconciled you really are to the pantheistic perspective you've sketched out, and I'm not sure just how honest you are about your description of choosing between the two buttons either. In your dream you did precisely the opposite, after all. You sacrificed the entire future of mankind so that you could live for a few miserable seconds more. On top of all that you showed yourself capable of killing your two travelling companions for their oxygen, just so that you could sit up there in your spaceship and watch yourself in the mirror of your own consciousness for a brief while.

☐ But that was a dream. Haven't you ever done anything in a dream that you wouldn't have done in reality?

☐ Of course, and I know you're a considerate person. It was touching how carefully you packed up and posted my bits and pieces. And you weren't mean at all, you were generous. I comforted myself with the thought that you'd at least kept the Volkswagen. That was never at issue, because I didn't have a driving licence. And you were the one who'd paid for the windscreen repair and the new headlights.

The old glass bell is on the windowsill in front of me, I'm picking it up now and ringing it. Can you hear?

☐ Yes! And I haven't forgotten Småland. There were two mute swans swimming side by side on that reedy little lake. You pointed them out and said they were you and me, that they were our own souls we could see on the glass-calm water. Do you remember? Then I put my arm round you and put forward another notion, but one that was just as keen and ardent. I said, They're the world soul. They don't know it themselves, but they're the world soul swimming out there.

I've always been a romantic about nature. You were as well. But you also felt *threatened* by it.

Berit's asleep. Are you going to write more tonight?

☐ I remember the swans. And I remember that we couldn't agree about what they symbolised. I'm going to write and send tonight, but don't struggle to stay awake. Just go to bed, Steinn, you can read it in the morning.

☐ Certainly not. We can sail through the night together.

☐ What did you say? I hope you've not been sitting there drinking!?!

☐ Calm down. I didn't say anything rude, did I? Just write away. I'm sure to be awake.

☐ I'll try to be succinct, because you know a lot of this already.

It was ages ago, when I was about ten or eleven and spending my summer holidays on Ytre Sula. One day a swallow hit the glass of Grandma's living-room window. Grandma thought we ought to wait a while before doing anything with the bird because sometimes, she said, birds that had crashed into windowpanes like that were only stunned and could wake up and take to the wing again fifteen minutes or half an hour later. She said that some birds got a new life, a life after death, because we could see that the bird was dead, but then suddenly it would be flying around again. But the day and the night passed, and the swallow didn't wake up; it was still lying there like a piece of litter next morning, and I had to bury it. I had to do it all on my own, my parents were in Bergen, and though I thought my grandmother could have helped, she said it was a child's job to bury dead birds; this experience was something you and I discussed several times in connection with those outbursts of mine.

But from then on, from the time I was ten or eleven, I grew up with the intense feeling that I was nothing more than a bedraggled bird myself, that I was *nature*. I was no longer a child. The carefree age of innocence was behind me.

Yes, Steinn, it *is* wonderful to think that children are being born who, for a good long while, will be able to live just for the moment, without the fear of death, without sorrow and anxiety. As far as I was concerned, part of my life ended when I was only ten or eleven; it certainly took a completely new turn. Long before I was sexually mature,

I was terrified and in a sense a little apart from this world – I was travelling away from it at all events.

Then I came to Oslo and met you. The time in between wasn't important, I recall it only as an endless round of piano lessons, tennis and homework, and in the final stage a bit of flirting and drunkenness. But you met me in my pain itself, because there was something wounded in you, or perhaps it was more like an aspect of earnestness. You realised, as I did, that there was no hope for the likes of us, apart from the immediate world around us. We were so naked, so defencelessly given over to one another and all the natural and ecstatic things we could overstimulate each other with – although these, at least for a time, could curb the thoughts of where we were ultimately headed.

But I always possessed a dualistic view of existence, which had been with me since that summer with Grandma. I felt that in the first instance we were souls, and that the physical desires which constantly welled up in us, although easily satisfied, were something quite different, something incidental to our masculinity or femininity, delightful in torrid moments, but which deep down we regarded as fickle and superficial. Didn't you find it that way too?

I would enjoy an ecstasy deeper than the deepest ocean

---

when on occasion you'd come up behind me, put your hand on my brow, breathe on my neck, gently lift my hair and whisper in my ear, Hello, soul! These were occasions when you wanted something other than sex, and they weren't that rare. Then, you know, it was my true soul you were talking to. You opened a door to a completely different register, to the spirit, and it was my soul that answered. Usually I just said, You ... That was enough. What else can you say to each other, soul to soul like that? I couldn't get closer to you than that.

Then I had those premonitions about you, Steinn. It's very important for me to remind you of those at this point. Often you would come back to our flat at Kringsjå half an hour before you actually arrived. The first few times I heard you coming, I was so sure it was you that I ran towards the front door to greet you, and sometimes also to entice you straight into the bedroom. Sometimes I'd have it all planned. But I learnt that it was only a premonition, that you were only on your way. So these premonitions had their uses. I had time to lay the table and make something nice to eat, or I could tidy myself up before trying to seduce you – I managed it every single time I made a serious effort. I'm sure you remember coming home to candlelight and a warm bedroom on certain winter evenings. You knew what was in store: you called it a love sauna and you laughed expectantly. But

I'm only writing about this now, Steinn, to remind you of my 'susceptibility' to what you now call the occult; it's been a living reality for me for at least as long as we've known each other.

Because that's not all. We woke up one May morning in 1976, not long before we went to the mountains to hike across the Jostedalsbreen glacier. I'd had a dream and turned to you in bewilderment. You immediately took fright because I was staring at you so intently. Was another outburst on the way?

'What is it?' you asked.

'I dreamt that Bjørneboe's dead,' I replied.

'Nonsense,' you said. You always thought such premonitions were nonsense.

'No, I know that Jens Bjørneboe is dead,' I reiterated. 'Steinn, he couldn't take any more.'

Then I started to cry. We had just read *The Dream and the Wheel* about the writer Ragnhild Jølsen. We'd read nearly all the novels Bjørneboe had written. You got cross. You went out into the kitchen and turned the radio on, and almost immediately there was a news bulletin. The main story was that Jens Bjørneboe was dead. Alarmed at that, you returned to bed and lay up close to me again.

You said, 'What are you *doing*, Solrun? Stop it! You're frightening me.'

*

Yes, I had those 'clairvoyant' experiences, and more often than I do now. But as your soul or your 'precursor' was always coming home half an hour before you arrived, and as I could have precognitive dreams, of which we could already see the clear proof the next morning, I gradually came to accept the idea that we human beings actually possess a free soul, I mean one independent of the body it inhabits at the moment.

On its own this still wasn't enough to reconcile me to my fate as a 'guest in reality'. I wept and you were brave, you put up with me. One September day I had an attack. I was to meet you outside the Sophus Bugge Auditorium, do you remember, after Edvard Beyer's Wergeland Lecture, and you comforted me as best you could. You just said, 'This evening you're going to be the belle of the Theatercafé.'

The Theatercafé was an expensive place for us, but it wasn't that long after we got our student loans, and we made an evening of it. I had *two* desserts! You were so nice. But you became more and more of a sceptic. I felt you turn cold. You were never unkind to me, but you developed into a cynic – I mean in the cognitive sense. Your bitterness took that path, and then, well, my bitterness took another path. The path of hope.

Telepathy, ESP or clairvoyance were genuine phenomena for me ever since I heard your first premonition. I heard you coming. But then you didn't come after all. And then you did come!

When we came across that book, the foundations had already been laid. So I wasn't totally unprepared when we met the Lingonberry Woman only a few hours later. I was at journey's end. There had to be an answer somewhere, a release ...

What is a person, Steinn? How often do you reflect that beneath that tissue-thin layer of sensitive skin on your thigh or forearm is *flesh* and *blood*? Have you ever tried to imagine what your insides and intestines look like? I mean from the inside! But is that *you*? Where would you locate the centre of yourself, the bit which says, thinks and dreams the *I*? In your gall bladder or your spleen? In your heart or your nerves? In your small intestine perhaps? Or should we instead search for that essence in the soul, in the spirit, in what *is*, because all the rest is nothing more than the ticking of a clock and grains of sand in an hourglass. Just so much chaff, if you ask me.

Now I'll jump back to our penultimate evening at the old hotel, the evening before the hotelier's daughter asked us to look after her three small girls for half an hour in the morning while she went to the bank.

We'd had our apple brandy and were about to go up to bed. But first we made a detour to the billiard room and had a game. It's strange to think that those same three ivory balls are still sitting there on the green baize. I wonder how many times they've clinked.

The billiard room was also the hotel's library and bar, and after I'd scored ten points and you'd only got eight, we went to the bookshelves as we'd done every afternoon or evening. They housed a very narrow, restricted selection of books, all of them pretty old, and the vast majority were about geography, geology and glaciology. But then – as if in unearthly counterpoint – I suddenly found *The Book of Spirits*, published in Christiania in 1893, only two years after the old hotel was built. It had been translated from French; the original title was *Le Livre des Esprits*, printed in Paris way back in 1857.

This was the evening before we met the Lingonberry Woman. Before we'd even left the billiard room we began to leaf through the book – quite likely I read a few sentences to you before we took it up to our room. There, to begin with we amused ourselves reading aloud to each other. For although a living person had edited the book, it was in fact one continuous manifesto of revelations from the spirit world. The book contained a collection of pronouncements from the spirits of the dead, communicated to the living during spiritualist seances. I remember how, right at the end of that evening, you put the book on the bedside table and said to me, 'I'd rather have one live woman in my arms than ten spirits in the bush.' And I fell for the flattery, I freely admit it. It was night-time.

But from that moment on something had been sown inside me. In the course of a few weeks I became a spiritualist, or a Christian spiritualist. It became my faith, and it became my solace, my comfort.

The next afternoon we met the Lingonberry Woman. It's a strange thought. But then, don't you think that once you've begun to open your mind to something, that something starts to open itself to you?

At any rate, no bird can fly into a house while the windows are shut. It'll just crash into the windowpane.

Once you've experienced such things as premonitions, telepathy, clairvoyance or precognitive dreams, it becomes clear to you that beyond the bodies that we temporarily inhabit, we're also souls that belong to a totally different *order* to the material one. As far as I was concerned, the road from that to a belief in the immortality of the soul was very short.

But how are things in Oslo at the moment? Are you asleep?

☐ No, I've been reading. It's almost two a.m. Are you still at your computer?

☐ Yes.

☐ It's almost unbelievable. You really *found* a salvation. You found a deliverance for your scared soul ... I could almost envy you, because I'm outside this new faith of yours, shivering out in the cold.

☐ But I haven't entirely given up bringing you inside. I *will* give you something, Steinn. I promise you. One day I'll convince you.

☐ And I won't prevent you from trying. Maybe I don't entirely believe in my own pantheism either. But now, perhaps, we ought to get to bed ...

☐ Yes, we'd better turn in now. Imagine you saying that *before* me for once.

☐ Good night!

☐ Good night!

Just one thing. I've set aside the whole of tomorrow for trying to re-narrate exactly what happened during that episode more than thirty years ago. I'll get some sleep first, then I'll settle down to it as early as possible tomorrow morning. I'll try to send several times during the day. If you can go round with the entire history of the universe

---

in your head, someone else can remember everything we experienced back then. Is that OK? Are we ready at last to put words to those events?

☐ We'll take the chance. We once promised each other never to refer to it again, but perhaps now we can release ourselves from that duty of silence.

Guess what I've been tippling all evening?

☐ Calvados! I can smell it from here. Distilled apples ...

☐ I'm impressed. You really *do* have some sixth sense after all. Sleep well. I'll hear from you in the morning.

☐ Sleep well!

VII

☐ One afternoon towards the end of May 1976 I was standing at our bedroom window in Kringsjå. The window was open, the weather was mild and I was breathing in the scent of spring. I didn't know whether it was the perfume of the new year I was inhaling or the sweetish-sour smell of last year's mould, but it couldn't have been the fresh buds on the trees, so I decided it must be the damp earth – the fertile soil from last year that was feeding the new shoots. I saw a boisterous magpie in some under-growth and a cat trying to scare it. The magpie put me in mind of the bird I'd had to bury in Solund, and once again I had that intense feeling of being ephemeral – it was beginning again, I was getting one of my attacks. First, tears welled up in my eyes, and all at once my head began to ache badly. Then I cried – I think the first thing I did was to let out an appalled groan. You'd realised what was happening because I could hear you entering the room. You passed *The Castle in the Pyrenees*, but before you managed to touch me, I'd turned quickly round and was

---

looking at you. 'One day we'll be dead!' I sobbed, or rather howled. Then I wept again, but allowed you to comfort me. Presumably you were thinking feverishly, and perhaps you realised that this time the offer of a paltry circuit or two of Lake Sognsvann wouldn't be enough. I think I remember the exact words you used just a moment after you put your arms around me – you used to twine my hair with one hand while pressing the other to the small of my back. There are many ways of holding a woman, and you had yours.

'Dry your tears now,' you said. 'We're going to ski across Jostedalsbreen.'

Half an hour later we were in the car, with our skis on the roof and our two rucksacks in the boot. The last time we'd done something mad was the cave-dweller project on the Hardangervidda plateau the summer before. Now the sun was high in the sky again, and it was a new season for escapades. I loved them. How I loved our escapades!

My moods could certainly change. We'd hardly put Oslo behind us before I was euphoric. You were too. We were so *happy*, Steinn! I said that no two people in the whole world knew each other better than we did. We'd lived together since we were nineteen, that was almost forever, all of five years, and we'd already told each other we were starting to get old. It's painful to think about it now, because we were still so very young and had our whole lives in front of us. That was thirty-one years ago.

We were driving the red Volkswagen, and as we cruised down towards Sundvollen we joked that as well as being man and woman we were also a couple of swallows weaving above the spruce tops and getting a bird's-eye view of the red Beetle. Do you remember? So we imagined seeing ourselves picking our way across the landscape with skis on the roof just a few days before the start of June. And we knew that at that very moment the world's purest harmony was to be found inside our red Volkswagen. We'd done two summers' work to pay for it.

Along Lake Krøderen and up Hallingdal we became sated with conversation – we'd talked about everything! – and after we passed Bromma we could go for a minute or even two without saying anything. But we were looking at the same things so it wasn't necessary to comment on all we saw. Once we sat there for fully four or five minutes without either of us saying a word, and then one of us burst out laughing, and the other fell about as well. That started us chattering again.

We'd driven on and on, but Hemsedal and western Norway still lay ahead of us. At the top of Hemsedal we saw a large articulated lorry with foreign plates in a lay-by on the right of the road. We talked about it many times in the week that followed. A few kilometres further on we noticed a woman walking near the road in the direction of the mountains, in the same direction as us. Look! you said. And then, Can you see?

It was late evening, and we thought it odd that a lone woman was out walking at that time of the day. The only reason we didn't stop to offer her a lift was that she wasn't walking on the road itself, but along a path a little to the right of the highway, and she was walking so purposefully too, across the moors to the mountains. She was wearing greyish clothes, and across her shoulders she had a rose-pink shawl. She made a picturesque sight, and the image of that woman with her pink shawl in the blue summer night has remained in my mind like a little video clip, as she walked with quick, resolute steps towards the mountains on some errand – no, she was going to *cross* the mountains, Steinn. She was headed for the west as well. You slowed down, and as we passed her, we both looked across. In the days that followed we agreed about what the woman had looked like. An older woman, we said. A middle-aged woman with a rose-pink shawl over her shoulders. Or we said a woman in her fifties . . .

But are you awake, Steinn? Did you get up early as well? During these hours while I'm in my yellow room writing to you today, you must be close to me. A whole generation ago we promised each other never to mention what happened up in the mountains again. But we're mutually absolved from that pact now.

172

☐ I'm here. It's the crack of dawn, but I'm already sitting in the kitchen with a double espresso. I'm reading your stuff as soon as you send it. I'll do that all day; I'll be online the whole time. In a moment I'll take my laptop to the office with me. I think it's the first time I've left home at this time of the morning – it's only just begun to get light. Berit's asleep, and I'm leaving a note to say I woke up early and couldn't get back to sleep. I said I've got lots to do.

But go on now, I'm on tenterhooks. You remember better than me.

☐ Up there at the top of Hemsedal you'd already got cross because we weren't likely to get a bed for the night, and then, just after we'd passed the woman with the shawl, you suddenly decided that you *wanted* me. At first it was just a jokey comment, casual talk I'd say, but gradually you got cheekier and more insistent, less casual, and I began to laugh again, but then you found a turn-off and drove a few metres down a forestry road next to the river. The weather was dry, and I thought you were going to entice me out into the heather between the trees. But it was cold, and you'd been getting definite notions about quite a different pièce de résistance. Poor you. For some unknown reason you'd got hooked on the fantasy of a certain type of acrobatics inside the red Beetle, and as you said, you couldn't free yourself from these intense flickering images. I'm only human, you said. I looked at you askance, you rolled your eyes and admitted, I'm only a man.

Half an hour later we were on the main road again, and you put on some speed. Spurred by sated desire it felt as if we were speeding through the air like a projectile. To the hills, to the hills! We'd registered that we were driving on Trunk Road 52, and we found that quite funny as we'd both been born in that year. Vintage Road, you said. Or perhaps I was the one who said it.

You were certainly the one behind the wheel the whole time, as I hadn't got a licence in those days. Perhaps it was midnight, but even then it wasn't completely dark at that time of year. The day had been hot, but now it was cooler and misty, and we were high up in the mountains. Had it been a dark autumnal night, the contours would have been sharper, and we would have seen more clearly in the light from the headlamps. Now everything was just mellow blue and dull insomnia. The only exception was a brilliant shimmer above the distant horizon. I think I commented on it – it was certainly something we remarked on in the ensuing days.

At Lake Eldrevatnet on the watershed and county boundary we suddenly caught sight of something red and fluttering in the twilight; we felt the car hit something and our seat belts tightened. You slowed down, or at least our speed dropped, but after a few moments you accelerated once more, and then there was an interval of some four or five minutes before either of us said anything. And surely that was the greatest mystery, because what were you thinking of, Steinn, and what was I thinking of? Although perhaps we weren't thinking at all. Perhaps we were just shocked.

After passing the long lake we met an oncoming white van crossing the mountains heading east, and then you said agitatedly, 'I think we've run someone over!'

It was as if we were thinking with one mind, for in that instant I thought it too. You turned towards me suddenly, and I nodded vigorously.

'I know,' I said. 'We ran into the woman with the rose-coloured shawl.'

We had passed Breistølen Mountain Hostel and soon arrived at the first sharp bend of the descent, and there at the bend you screeched to a halt and turned round. You didn't say anything, but I could tell from your shoulders and the tense look on your face what you were thinking: Perhaps she needs help. Perhaps she's seriously injured. Perhaps we've killed someone . . .

A few minutes later we were back at the place where the car had collided with something in the dim light. You stopped and we both jumped out. It was cold and there was a light breeze. But we couldn't see anyone. You discovered that the nearside headlight was smashed and you picked up some glass splinters from the road and ditch. We looked about us, and suddenly you pointed down at a pink shawl spread lightly across the heather on the ground sloping down to the lake, only a couple of metres from the car and the road. The shawl looked quite clean and fresh, as if it had just been lifted off a woman's shoulders, and it fluttered gently in the wind, almost as if it were alive. Neither of us dared to touch it; we just looked around, and even though it was a summer night we couldn't make out a human shape in any direction. We had nothing but a rose-pink shawl to go on. You found a couple more splinters from the headlamp, and then we drove off. Fast.

Once again we were in shock. You were trembling as you pressed the accelerator and held the steering wheel, and I don't think either of us said anything, but our souls were so intertwined that we could read each other's thoughts and feelings.

In the hours and days that followed we analysed it all thoroughly, but even as we sat in the red Beetle, it was clear to us we'd run over the mysterious woman that we'd seen on the moors just before enjoying our little moment of fun down by the river. By stopping, we'd given her a fatal head start.

The only sign of her now was the pink shawl. So we both thought that the injured or dead woman must have been picked up from the side of the road and taken away in the white van. That, we decided, was the only possible explanation for her disappearance. It was years before mobile phones, and our minds were full of images of the driver of the white van either stopping to get help at the first farm in Hemsedal, and of course ringing for both police and ambulance, or electing to put his foot down and get the victim of our overconfidence to the hospital at Gol. But the thought also crossed our minds that there might be no reason to drive hell for leather. The driver of the white van might be making his pensive and solemn way to the police station in Hemsedal to deliver a dead woman he'd found on Trunk Road 52. There he might mention the oncoming Volkswagen too.

The road descended towards the west, and when we'd passed Breistølen for the second time and arrived at the sharp corner where we'd turned round, you stopped abruptly at the precipice and ordered me out of the car. Out! was all you shouted. Out!

You were frenzied. I thought maybe you were evil and that now you wanted to injure me; at any rate I didn't dare contradict you, so I loosened my seat belt and got out of the car. Steinn, Steinn, I wept. What are you going to do now? Are you just going to leave me here? I was so shaken that I thought, Is he going to kill me? To get rid of the only witness? Maybe he's killed before … Then you revved up the engine and set off towards the precipice. Were you going to drive off the road and end it all? I cried out again: Steinn! Steinn! But you just crashed the car into a block of stone on the edge of the precipice. Resolutely, you got out of the car and checked that the right-hand headlamp was also smashed, the bumper was bent too, almost right back on itself.

'Why did you do that?' I asked.

And you didn't even look up at me.

But you said, 'This was where we had a slight accident with the car.'

You fetched the glass shards we'd brought with us from the mountain and placed them in front of the block next to the new glass splinters. It was as if you were putting the finishing touches to a jigsaw puzzle.

It was the middle of the night and cold. I thought perhaps the car wouldn't start, but luckily it was still serviceable if a bit rattly. We'd been tired and lost concentration and had driven into the big block of stone which must have been placed on the corner as a barrier against the sheer drop.

We drove down to Borgund and started as the old stavechurch suddenly rose out of the misty morning light like some macabre stage set. It was surrounded by ancient gravestones, and before one of these burnt a candle – rose-pink in the muted summer night.

We drove on by the side of the river as it got lighter, and paradoxically that morning we got more jumpy the lighter it became. It was almost day by the time we reached

Lærdal, but we agreed that it was both too late and too early to try to get a bed; it would also arouse suspicion, and we had no desire to display the battered car, so we drove the last ten kilometres to the ferry at Revsnes. There, with several hours until the first ferry, we took up position on the quay – the only car there – and decided to tip the seats back and try to get forty winks. But really we'd resigned ourselves. We said that the police would surely come for us before we'd crossed the fjord. There was nowhere to go until the ferry came. Even if the woman were dead, and even if she weren't able to explain, the driver of the white van had seen a red Volkswagen with skis on its roof only minutes before he'd found an injured or dead woman in the ditch. It was obvious that the police could arrive at any time.

Why had she been walking high up in the mountains in the middle of the night? There were no buildings up there, not even a fishing hut or a hunting lodge. She hadn't been particularly well dressed, and wasn't wearing anything resembling hiking clothes.

Who *had* that woman been? Could we be sure that she'd been alone up there? Or had she been with others? Perhaps she was mixed up in something. After all we'd noticed the large articulated lorry at the top of Hemsedal. Perhaps something was afoot . . .

*

We were far too keyed up to manage any sleep. The light scared us. We lay there with our eyes closed whispering together like kids on a sleepover. I mentioned that we'd only moved a couple of degrees on a small planet orbiting a sun, and you quickly added that the sun was only one of a hundred thousand million other stars in the Milky Way. And so we were off. What we'd experienced was no more than a ripple on a great ocean. We had to enlarge the perspective. We had to take the focus off ourselves. But now I didn't find my eyes filling with tears and blurting out that one day we'd no longer be here. It was inappropriate now: it was no longer the right climate for sorrow; guilt had taken sorrow's place, because now we might well have caused the death of another human being. It was so awful to think about that I didn't dare articulate it. But it went through my mind the whole time. Taken a life! I, who couldn't even manage to accept my own unconscious absence one day from the surface of the planet and thus from the whole gigantic universe, from everything. From you too, Steinn, from you too.

After that fragile morning on the ferry quay, I think there were hardly any occasions during the next few days when we mentioned 'the woman we ran over' or made any other direct reference to what had happened. We just said *it*, if we had to refer to the subject, or *what happened*. But you were driving extremely fast up there on the mountain plateau; we'd just come down a gentle incline; you'd put your foot to the floor and made the little Beetle do all she was capable of, and then we'd possibly knocked down and killed a woman on Hemsedalsfjellet. We just couldn't talk about it afterwards. From the moment we were back home in Oslo, that part of the story was buried and suppressed. So how could we manage to live together? Living together is partly to do with talking to each other, of thinking aloud together, of fooling around and laughing, and also sleeping together and being close to each other.

On the other hand, we talked about the Lingonberry Woman quite openly to begin with, and she's the one who today, so many years later, enables me to repeat almost without a trace of shame that we managed to knock down and kill someone on that mountain. I'll come back to that wonderful Lingonberry Woman, don't worry. But this once I want to make sure I relate everything in chronological order.

And you? Have you managed to get to the office?

☐ I have indeed, and it wasn't many minutes after I'd logged on to Outlook that I received the day's first email. It was from you, and now I've read and deleted it.

You remember more of the details than me. The only thing I wonder if you're exaggerating is your emphasis on how even then we had definite notions that the woman we'd hit wasn't just injured, but had actually died in the collision. She could have had a bad knock and broken an arm, and could for that matter have got a lift in the white van back to Hemsedal. But the event was dramatic enough, and now I've sat here in my office and relived the whole thing.

I agree that you ought to wait before introducing the 'Lingonberry Woman'. I'll certainly have some divergent opinions. But you know that anyway.

□ Divergent opinions! I can almost smell that scientific institute around you. What does it look like, by the way? Your office, I mean ...

□ I'm sitting in a typical university hole in the wall, a rectangular office in the mathematics block, also known as the Niels Henrik Abel Building, the shelves, desk and floor of which are piled high with scientific reports, compendiums and journals. But today I'm paying hardly any attention to these mundane surroundings. As I read what you've written on the screen, it's as if I'm sitting in the same room listening to you narrate, or even in the same car. So carry on. We'd parked on that ferry quay on the southern shore of Sognefjord.

□ It was already daylight by about four o'clock, and a little later the sun rose, but we kept our eyes tight shut and continued whispering. We reminded each other how secure it had been to live in the Stone Age, both the one several thousand years ago and the one on the Hardangervidda plateau the year before. Even that last one now seemed unimaginably distant from what we'd gone through that night. We dreamt our way back to those long nights when we could lie outside the cave and gaze out into the universal night. We thought we could see across such huge distances then, we gazed right across the miracle of space. It was almost painful to have such close contact with so many pinpricks of light-years-distant glow all at once. Those exotic lights, our optical neighbours in spite of everything, had hurtled through space for thousands of years before they reached our minds and had been received and muted there. The rays from those distant celestial bodies had travelled on and on before they touched our retinas – continuing their journey into a new dimension and another fairy tale, through the veil of sensory apparatus and right down to the depths of the soul. Then one night the moon appeared, first as a knife-sharp sickle, but waxing with each passing night until eventually it flooded both the Hardangervidda plateau and the vault of the sky with its silvery sheen. It came as a relief, and not simply because we could look into one another's eyes at night as well, but because it provided a respite for our eyes and our souls from gazing into those depths of space, as we had done up till then.

While we sat in the red Beetle mumbling about the Stone Age, the universe and our distant past, we still had our eyes closed and it was night – we'd decided it would remain a sleepover for as long as possible, regardless of whether it was the police or the ferry crew who came to wake us – but when we heard the distant drone of the ferry out in the fjord, we knew that the night would soon be over, and so one of us would have to be quick to remember the enormous shower of shooting stars the evening we slaughtered the lamb. It had been so spectacular, we'd said nothing. We had counted thirty-three shooting stars in the space of a couple of minutes, but we'd been so dumbfounded that we hadn't the presence of mind to think out the ninety-nine wishes that were ours. But we'd had a good meal. We'd already eaten roast lamb, and had more set aside for the coming days. And wishes? Well, we had each other.

We crossed the fjord. The ferrymen looked critically at the front of the car and then sympathetically at us. It's the same with accidental damage as it is with physical injury: you can tell when it's recent. Witnesses, we thought. I think we whispered something of the sort to each other. Even in those days the Norwegian Broadcasting Corporation's night-time service had a brief news summary every hour. We knew that. What we didn't know was what they were listening to just then up in the wheelhouse.

––––––

But we were waved ashore at Kaupanger and continued our westward drive towards Hella. From there we'd take a boat up to Fjærland, which would be our starting point for the trip up to the glacier. This was long before the Internet, but we'd brought along the *Norwegian Timetable Guide* and we knew that we'd only just have time to make the first ferry to Fjærland, and if we didn't catch that, we'd have to spend half the day waiting at Hella. But then the game was up: we were stopped by the police between Hermansverk and Leikanger. They'd caught up with us at last.

Two police cars were standing there, one with flashing blue lights. I thought how idiotic it had been to imagine we could get away with it so easily: the whole car front was clear evidence of what we'd been involved in. Now it was broad daylight and even without mobile phones it must have been hours since the police had been informed about what had happened. Although you'd carefully faked an alibi back at the precipice, you were the one who admitted, loud and clear, when we were waved into the side of the road, We give up. We're not going to deny a thing.

I nodded and nodded. But still you went on: We just panicked, you see, that was all. And I nodded again. I was so tired and miserable. Everything was ruined. Everything I loved and believed in had been trampled underfoot. After what had happened on the mountain, I had no will but yours.

But it was only a routine check. We didn't even have to get out of the car, and that was lucky because I certainly wouldn't have been able to stand up. It was early Monday morning, but there was no breathalyser either. But we did get a ticket. We were told to repair the headlights within ten days, by which time, as the police said, we'd be back in Oslo. They were kind and considerate, but although the light summer nights had already arrived, the ticket contained a condition about not driving at night until the lights were working again.

An admonition not to drive at night, Steinn. That was all we got. And it was a decision that we really couldn't argue with . . .

We made Hella in good time before the ferry left. Hella, like Revsnes, was a typical non-place; it was just a ferry stage, and there wasn't even a kiosk. My unquenchable yearning for chocolate had returned and I was suffering. So there was nothing to talk about during the half-hour before the boat arrived from Vangsnes except our skis. We would park the Volkswagen there – we agreed about that. It would be pointless taking it with us to a fjord village with practically no roads, and it wasn't much fun to show off any more. But our skis?

I'm sure you remember all this as well as I do, but this story has to be related once in a coherent way.

Then we talked things over sensibly, calculated. Should

---

we turn round? But out there on that granite headland we were in thorough agreement that we owed it to each other to get to the glacier. That was where we'd been going; we'd promised one another and, no matter what happened after that, we had to find a place to sleep – we needed a duvet to crawl under together. But whether it would be one or two or three days before we were picked up, we had no way of knowing. We were certain only that it was a matter of time, of days at best. We'd seen how the crew of the ferry had noted the recent signs of collision on the car, and we'd been stopped, inspected and recorded by a regular police check. The rest, we agreed, was a matter of coordination and investigation, i.e. of time. But we knew in that half-hour at Hella that there'd be no ski trip up the glacier. We weren't cold-blooded enough to set out on a glacier hike after what had happened. We'd have to read the papers and listen to the radio. We were on our guard, we had to be. And we knew of a legendary hotel we could stay at out there. The skis could stay at Hella in that case. But no, the description was a red Volkswagen with two pairs of skis on its roof. At the end of May! It was too risky. And how were we going to pass ourselves off out there? The most plausible idea was to arrive as glacier hikers.

Something within us registered that no matter how it ended – in terms of the police or their investigation, I mean – we as a couple had probably suffered a severe blow. Apart from my panic attacks and your tendency to have a drink or two too much, we'd lived together almost free of friction right up to the moment the woman with the rose-pink shawl had been run over at Lake Eldrevatnet, and now for the first time we'd been plunged into crisis. But as yet we couldn't let go of each other. Tomorrow perhaps, or the next day, but not yet.

We had to have a few final hours and days together before it was all emphatically over.

And so it was in an almost light-hearted mood that we made the boat trip up the narrow arm of the fjord. We travelled due north towards the huge glacier. The view made such a strong impression that something happened between us: it was like a release, or like a dam that suddenly bursts. We began to fool about and laugh again. Do you remember? We thoroughly lived out our parts as free and untroubled people. We were marvellous actors. We hadn't slept, and that certainly helped, but more important was the fact that we were still uninhibited together – as we might be for another twelve or twenty-four, or maybe as much as forty-eight hours more. Suddenly we were Bonnie and Clyde. We were used to being something apart, an outpost as we often called it. Now we were outlaws as well. We took on the roles – it's something we can admit to more than thirty years later – we began to take on the roles of cynics.

*

At the hotel we simply said we wanted to stay a few days, we didn't know exactly how long, but we said we wanted to go up on the glacier as they'd seen the skis, and we lied about having done a glacier course and some glacier hiking. You mentioned something about the Svartisen glacier . . .

But we simply wanted a few days together, you and I. We thought that it might be our last escapade. Didn't we claim to be newly-weds? This was only four years after the so-called 'concubinage law' had been repealed; even during our first year together our unmarried status could have been reported to the police as an 'offensive and indictable' relationship.

At any rate, we asked for their best room. We said we had something special to celebrate – I think we spun some yarn about passing exams, and that was true as far as it went, because I'd just finished my subsidiary history of religion course and you'd taken some credits in physics.

Getting their best room was no problem, because it wasn't yet high season. We got the Tower Room, and Steinn, I hesitate to mention this in my story, but it was the same room that Niels Petter and I happened to be given when we arrived that night in the summer. It was strange being there again – with him. Just how accidental it was that we chanced on that room I'm not sure, and now I'm not talking about anything occult, but he was the one who'd made the booking, and I'm married to a very open-handed and considerate man. He was upset that you took up almost all of our visit to the Book Town. We'd looked forward to going round the bookshops and hunting for all the books we hadn't managed to read when we were young, but I think I told you that he perked up on the way home.

While we were standing at reception checking into the hotel that morning we also, rather cheekily perhaps, made another request. We didn't have any choice. We enquired if there was a radio in the room, and when they said there wasn't we asked if we could borrow a transistor radio. Perhaps that was risky, but we felt desperately short of information. We said that you were studying law and were keen to follow some of the current affairs programmes. Something about West Germany and the Baader-Meinhof gang, I told them.

Ulrike Meinhof had been found dead in Stammheim Prison only a few days before. I don't know why I said what I did, but it may have been because suddenly I felt that we two had a little of Andreas Baader and Ulrike Meinhof about us. You gave me an annoyed look.

But we got the room and the radio. We had our own semicircular balcony with a fantastic view of the glacier, the fjord and the two shops down by the old steamship quay. But when we went to bed in our hotel room that morning, we just lay there listening to the radio. We didn't even look at the time because we were almost certain that everything on that small transistor set would be about us. Before we succumbed to sleep, we managed to find a regular news bulletin, with news from both home and abroad. Parliament had given its support to a bill to reduce the age of military service from twenty to nineteen years of age, and the German philosopher Martin Heidegger was dead. But there was no news from the mountains.

This absence of information had already begun to trouble us. Fresh in our minds from the champagne seminars in our double bed at home was Dostoyevsky's Raskolnikov, and like him we'd started to entertain a certain desire to be found out, or at least to be discreetly reprimanded or questioned. But we fell asleep instantly. I don't think we even switched off the radio, and we didn't wake up again until late in the afternoon.

I was woken by your crying. Now you were the one who was crying. I comforted you. I laid my arm across your chest, kissed your neck and tried to rock you.

Shortly afterwards we were sitting up in bed again listening to the radio. We hung on every word of a half-hourly news bulletin. But there was nothing. It was now seven o'clock, and more than half a day had passed since the incident in the mountains, an incident that looked very like a brutal hit-and-run murder in which the callous perpetrator had left the scene of the crime – and the injured or dead victim – without calling for an ambulance or reporting to the police. 'Large police reinforcements have today been deployed ...' But no, there was nothing like that. Even though we, ensconced in our hotel room at the upper end of an arm of Sognefjord, knew full well that we had driven away from, and deserted, the woman with the rose-pink shawl. Totally intoxicated by our own happiness, we had mown her down and then simply continued on our way. We did find her shawl. So it must have been the driver of the white van who'd picked up the pieces after us. But hadn't he contacted the police?

What was all this? Why weren't they broadcasting what had happened? Why was it being hushed up? There must be some reason for it. What *could* the explanation be? Why wouldn't the authorities say what they knew? What was that mysterious woman in her grey clothes and pink shawl doing up in the mountains in the middle of the night? Why was she there? Could there be some military or secret-service involvement? Could we accidentally have got mixed up in something big, something that touched on national security?

I was the one with the livelier imagination. Could we be certain that the woman we'd run down really was an ordinary person? I asked. There was nothing about a missing person on the radio. The police hadn't appealed for witnesses. Perhaps she was an alien, a visitor from outer space? Because there *had been* a strange light over the mountains that night, I coaxed, trying to get you to say something. I said we'd seen a brilliant light in the sky.

We found the whole thing totally perplexing. Who was the victim? If she wasn't an alien or some kind of spectre, someone somewhere must be asking who the perpetrator was. We tried to construct a profile: they'd have to be looking for a man, no doubt about that – a woman would never have just run away from something like that. Perhaps for some reason the police or the security police wanted to try to find the offender before going public and announcing what had happened.

The car was parked at Hella. Should we simply report ourselves? We could phone in an anonymous tip about the pranged car at the ferry quay, and then our intolerable behaviour would finally be brought to an end. The car was already registered as a suspect vehicle in police files.

But out of this chaos of questions and tentative answers a new, coldly calculating ambition was born. I was the one who articulated it first. I said, Dear Steinn. We've lived together for five years. Suddenly we've been very unlucky and for once we've done something really silly together, because it wasn't sensible just to drive on like that after the collision. But whatever happened to the poor woman we ran over, we can't help her now. So shouldn't we just try to make these final days as lovely as we can?

Sirius, I was pleading. Andromeda, Steinn! And you got

the association at once, I mean to what we'd been talking about back at Revsnes.

I pleaded for us, and you weren't difficult to win over. And so began those marvellous, final days we had together. We had a shower, and half an hour later we were sitting down in the museum-like lounge with an aperitif. They didn't have Golden Power. But they did have Smirnoff and lime.

After dinner we sat in front of the fire in the lounge again with our coffee, but from then on and for the remainder of the week we had the radio schedule in our minds, and we had to go up to our room to hear the news at ten o'clock. But still there was nothing.

I don't need to go into details about the week we spent together up there, because you remember it, and we talked a bit about it the last time we met. But we went for long walks every day. On the first day we plodded up Supphelledal and right up to the glacier tongue. Can you remember everything from that day, Steinn? Do you remember what we found in the moss down by the river after we'd eaten our chocolate and bought some home-knitted mittens at Hjørdis' souvenir shop right by the Supphellebreen glacier? Perhaps we should let that remain a secret between the two of us. Next day we borrowed bicycles and from then on we explored Horpedal and Bøyadal. In Bøyadal we spent several hours on the moraine left by the Little Ice Age watching the glacier calve.

We took the small transistor radio with us on all our hikes. Once as we passed reception a woman called Laila pointed to it and asked with just a hint of sarcasm, 'Baader-Meinhof?'

We pretended not to hear. But the lack of news persisted. Nobody bothered about what Bonnie and Clyde had done on their wild ride across the country. And we enjoyed it because it gave us another day. We had no greater time-scale. We delighted in every hour we were granted.

We discussed and speculated. Could that female have been *meant* to be run over by a car and killed? That would reduce our feelings of guilt a bit, but the thought of it made us feel used. Maybe she'd been pushed into the road just as we drove past, because it was almost light and yet we'd seen nothing until suddenly there was something red in front of the bonnet. Nor did we see if there was anyone in the bushes when we returned to the scene. Or might she have been dead even before the car struck her? Why not? Well, why not? All we saw was 'something red in front of the bonnet', a phrase we'd used many times, but we hadn't been aware of the woman herself, so perhaps it was only her shawl we'd seen, in the light air up there, in the wind. Someone had already killed her and only needed to stage a fatal accident to conceal another crime. Perhaps she'd been lying on the roadside, and without the rose-pink shawl on her shoulders she hadn't been easy to spot. Although the collision with her had been sufficient to smash a headlamp ...

She was a foreigner! We'd convinced ourselves of this after a while. That was why no one had reported her missing. And we'd seen a foreign articulated lorry, too – we suddenly agreed it was German – a little below the summit of Hemsedal just before ... well, just before you wanted to go up that forestry road, Steinn.

Perhaps the lorry driver had picked her up. Or perhaps there was a link between the lorry and the white van. It all happened in the middle of the night. Certain meetings do take place in the middle of the night.

We began to ramble on about a German lorry that had crossed the country and a woman in her fifties – maybe she was a courier – who was crossing the mountains to meet a van on the other side. But even with our intense powers of speculation, we got no further ...

But are you there?

☐ Yes, and I think you took your time replying. I've done little else today except wait for emails from you. I was pacing about like a wild animal in a cage waiting for you to contact me. This office is tiny. But gradually I calmed down and began to get on with something practical. I've tidied up a whole pile of papers and theses, the sort of chore one does every five years. I've also begun to feel a particular kind of restlessness tug at me. But go on with the story now, and don't feel pressurised by my impatience into telling things too briefly or too fast.

☐ Those 'final days' before they'd track us down seemed endless, and it was an especially romantic week because we were living at such a pitch, not knowing how long our happiness would last. But in a way the uncertainty was also impossible to live with. Grateful as we were for our 'week of grace', as one of us called it on the last day, we began to talk with some anticipation about how western Norway's answer to Bonnie and Clyde would be seen. We imagined the stories in the newspapers; we talked about the headlines. The idea that we might go scot-free and that our misdemeanour would never catch up with us didn't even strike us as a possibility. I don't really know, but I wouldn't be surprised if, had we realised that we might live the rest of our lives with what had happened as an unexplained mystery, we'd have been horrified at the prospect. For what was unbearable was not knowing all the time. Almost a week had passed, still there was no word on the news that a woman had been run over on the pass, and been cruelly and heartlessly deserted that night at the scene of the accident on Hemsedalsfjellet.

Who was that woman, Steinn!!!

*

We had a bit of a problem explaining things to our hosts at the pleasant hotel. Why didn't we go up on the glacier as we'd said we would? You said I wasn't on top form, and I nodded dutifully as you lied about my migraines. After fleeing from a traffic accident, and possibly from a dead or seriously injured woman, it was easy to lie. We were waiting for a bit, we explained. We sort of pretended I'd got a period. But I hadn't. Perhaps you think it's strange that I'm recalling this now. But we never had one below-par day, and I've never suffered from migraines. We did everything so much as a pair that I thought it beastly of you to blame me.

One day our nice hostess at the hotel asked us, jokingly or half-jokingly, if we'd run away or were hiding from something. Do you remember what we said? We were both tongue in cheek. We've run away from anything that smacks of responsibility, we said. We're hiding from every kind of hustle and bustle. She looked at us suspiciously, scrutinising us. That made us a little unsure, and you became a bit sharper. You said, Well, isn't this a holiday destination?

This was on our way in to breakfast, and during the meal we agreed that it was about time to leave. It wasn't simply because of the questions. The biggest pull on us was simply to revisit the spot where the accident had happened. They say that the criminal returns to the scene of his crime, and we had a good reason. We had to see if there were any clues we'd overlooked. And particularly if the rose-pink shawl was still lying there.

And there was something else as well. I had woken before you that morning, and when you got out of bed you found me stretched on the old chaise longue deeply immersed in the book I'd found in the billiard room and which we'd been reading bits out of the previous evening. I'm referring to *The Book of Spirits*, which you'd labelled a 'spiritualistic book of revelations'. Now you flared up immediately, almost worked yourself into a fury, and I hardly know why, but I suspected you of wanting to leave that morning just to part me from my new reading material. The book should have been returned before departure, but without you knowing I stowed it in my pack and didn't remove it again until we were back in Oslo.

But as we were going through the lounge on our way out to the balcony, to see the fjord and the copper beeches that last morning, the hotel owner's daughter, the woman who runs it today, asked us whether we could look after her three young daughters while she went out to the bank, if we had half an hour to spare that morning. Of all things, the small fjord community had a bank branch. We answered yes straight away. The girls were sweet – we already knew them well – the youngest wasn't more than two, and during the previous couple of months I'd begun to talk seriously about stopping my contraceptive pill. We were grateful for the confidence now placed in us, for who would have allowed Bonnie and Clyde to be babysitters? I can't remember why any more, but it ended up with us looking after the girls for almost the entire morning, and we said it was the least we could do in return for the loan of the transistor radio and the bikes. We didn't really need to say that. The fact was that we'd already spent a small fortune at the hotel. We were good customers and neither stinted on wine with our meals or on something with our coffee afterwards. They had Calvados, Steinn! Your memory is quite correct. In those days it was a rarity, at least in small hotels outside the big cities. But after our car trip to Normandy we'd fallen in love with Calvados. I can't remember now whether it was even stocked by the state-run off-licences in the middle of the 70s, but anyway it would have been way beyond our means under normal circumstances. But out here, amongst the deep scars of several ice ages, we sat and drank Calvados each evening after our meal.

So we spent another day at the hotel. About noon, when our stint with the girls was over, we found ourselves with a final afternoon to ourselves. We had explored almost every corner of the small fjord settlement; we'd scaled a couple of the nearby peaks – to which our knees bore witness the morning afterwards – but oddly enough we hadn't been to the shepherd's hut up the valley directly behind the hotel. Provided the car was still parked at Hella and hadn't been towed away to be investigated by the police, we'd be driving home the next morning, or at least as far east as we could get. We took nothing for granted. But we had one hike left to do, and today the walk was to the shepherd's hut. The weather was magnificent; we'd hardly had any rain during our stay.

With a packed lunch and a Thermos of tea we were soon making our way up Mundalsdal, where you and I walked again only a few weeks ago. I'm sure you remember everything from both those occasions, but now I'll put down all I remember myself so that you'll have to think carefully through what happened one more time.

We passed the last farm on the left with its red barn and the rifle range on the right, while the road continued for some distance on the right-hand side of the delightful River Mundalselven and finally arrived at the summer farm of Heimstølen. In places we had to jump across the sheep muck and cowpats on the gravel track, the animals had just been turned out to graze for the summer.

We were enjoying ourselves. A week had passed and we didn't know what lay ahead. Even if it did turn out that the event up there on Hemsedalsfjellet never caught up with us, we were scarred for life, we realised that, and we didn't know how we'd manage to live together with the memories of what we'd gone through. But we were still joking and laughing, we were still the same, and we realised with a certain tinge of melancholy that this was our last day in paradise, in this 'erotic backwater' as we put it, although it wasn't the backwater that was erotic so much as the two of us who'd been frolicking about in it for the past week.

And as we walked, you wanted to fondle me the whole time. At one point you even demanded more, and you meant it, it wasn't just talk. We've got the whole valley to ourselves, you cajoled, it's easy to hide in an alder thicket and it's warm, but I was stern and said that we'd go up to the shepherd's hut first. Once we'd done that, I remarked lightly, then we'd see how much of a man you were. I remember that line, because it annoyed you so. But then something happened that unmanned you totally in the days, even in the weeks, that followed. The truth is that we were never together again after that. We've never had intercourse since.

A thick clump of foxgloves was growing in the ditch on the left side of the track a couple of hundred metres from Heimstølen. *Digitalis purpurea*. They were so tall and rose-pink. I knew that you could die from eating them, but I also knew that foxglove leaves could save people from death. There was something alluring about the bell-shaped flowers. I tore myself loose from you and ran across to touch them. Come on! I said.

We concentrated on the foxgloves for a short while, but

then our attention was directed towards a dense stand of birches on the right, gently sloping down to the track. There was a small clearing amongst the black and white trunks, a bright green patch of moss, and there, suddenly, was a woman in grey clothes with a rose-pink shawl across her shoulders; it was precisely the same colour as the foxgloves. It's something I've thought about a great deal since, in the intervening years.

She was looking fixedly at us and smiling. She was the woman we'd run over on Hemsedalsfjellet, Steinn. It felt as if she'd suddenly been planted in the landscape by a higher being in our honour. Today I think I know more about who she was and where she came from. But wait!

Afterwards we were in complete agreement about what we'd seen. We agreed that it was the woman we'd seen hiking a few metres from the main road at the top of Hemsedal barely a week before. She was wearing the same shawl, the one that was still up there by the mountain lake, and she was the same person. So we were quite united about what we saw. The odd thing was that we couldn't agree about what she *said*. It was really strange and at the time it seemed quite extraordinary, although even that I have a reasonable explanation for now.

Well, what did she say? I remember perfectly clearly that she turned towards me and said, 'You are what I was, and I am what you will become.' But you insisted that she'd said something quite different. Wasn't that very peculiar after we'd agreed again and again that what we'd *seen* was identical? You stubbornly maintained that she'd looked at you and said, 'You should have got a speeding ticket, my lad.'

After all, the statements don't sound similar. Nor are the meanings anything like the same. 'You are what I was, and I am what you will become,' and then, 'You should have got a speeding ticket, my lad.' You picked up certain words and I picked up quite different ones. But why should she give us a double message? And how did she manage that trick? That was the greatest mystery then. But wait . . .

Today I'm certain that the 'elderly woman with the rose-pink shawl' was the same one we ran over and killed and who now came to us from the other side. And she came to comfort us! She smiled, and although I wouldn't go as far as to say it was a warm smile, because words like 'warm' and 'cold' have rather human connotations, it certainly wasn't unpleasant. It was roguish, playful and mischievous. No, it was seductive, Steinn. Come, come, come! it said. There is no death. So come, come, come! Then she simply faded away and was gone.

You knelt down on the track, covered your face with your hands and cried. You didn't want to look me in the eyes, but I bent over you and rocked you again.

―――――

'Steinn,' I said, 'she's gone now.'

But you just went on sobbing. I was terrified as well, because I didn't believe in anything myself in those days, but having my man to look after helped me a bit.

Suddenly you jumped up and began running up the valley. You were running for dear life, and I tried to keep up with you. I couldn't let you get away from me. Soon we were walking side by side again, and after a while we began talking about what had happened to us. We were both equally agitated.

We hadn't yet begun to take positions. We questioned one another, we discussed, we weighed pros and cons. But we were in agreement that the woman we'd seen in the birch copse was the same person we'd seen on Hemsedalsfjellet, and whom we'd subsequently run over and, as I thought, killed – it was now definite, there was no room for further doubt – even though you later argued even more vociferously that not only had she survived, but that she'd clearly coped extremely well.

How did she manage to follow us? you asked appalled. You were scared that she was still on our heels. You thought she might have checked in at the hotel and were worried we might meet her again at dinner. Your fears moved more and more on to firm, materialistic ground. I slowly began to test out a completely different point of view. I doubted she'd got a room at the hotel, or that we'd see her at dinner. She died, Steinn, I said. You looked at me, weighing me up. And I went on, Maybe she didn't come *after* us. Maybe she simply came *to* us. From the other side, Steinn. You stared. But there was no power in your glance. Just helplessness.

☐ Yes, it was helplessness. I knew we were going to drift apart. I couldn't then believe – and I can't today – that the dead are capable of visiting us, or that they can be found at all, anywhere. You could, and now I'm capable of respecting your views, so in spite of it all something has changed over the years, but you're right: at the time I couldn't.

But please carry on. I think you're being faithful to our story.

I've been getting more and more restless and fidgety after pacing my tiny office for much of the morning. I feel I've got to do something, it's now midday, and I've made a decision.

Write the final chapters now. I'm pretty sure I know how they'll come out, because we talked about it extensively before you suddenly cut all ties and went home to Bergen. I'll reply before the day is out, I promise.

☐ When we were up at the shepherd's hut we agreed that we'd forget about any interpretation for as long as possible. Next day we'd have a long drive home, and we'd also be crossing the mountains at that county boundary again. Shouldn't we for the moment just come to an agreement about what we'd actually experienced while it was still fresh in our minds?

We agreed that I had squatted down and touched the rose-coloured flowers. Then you came up behind me, first just caressing my hair, but then you got down and touched the foxgloves as well. I couldn't quite remember if it was something we *heard* on the other side of the road at that point or not, but certainly something made us turn suddenly. At that instant the figure of a woman materialised between the birch trunks, standing on the moss with her rose-pink shawl across her shoulders, 'like the lingonberry woman in a fairy tale'. Those were my words. I was the one who introduced the name, and it helped us express ourselves – it became a verbal plank to which two needy souls could cling. For many days we managed to talk about the Lingonberry Woman, and it seems that we still can more than thirty years later. We couldn't then have spoken so easily about an encounter with a ghost or an apparition, or about a spirit that had appeared to us. We must remember, this was the middle of the 1970s. It was just a few days after Ulrike Meinhof had been found dead in Stammheim Prison, and novels with titles like *Jenny's Got the Sack, Keep On, Into Your Time, The Iron Cross, Campaign* and *Graffiti* were being published in Norway that year. Of course there were a few lonely voices who proclaimed that we were entering an entirely new era, that we were at a turning point and now stood on the threshold of the 'Age of Aquarius'.

Your materialistic standpoint – in contrast to my dawning spiritualism – caused you to come up with an amusing theory in your febrile search for understanding. We'd agreed that the Lingonberry Woman was identical to the woman we'd seen on Hemsedalsfjellet. Suddenly you said, Try to view it as a film, or try to read it as a crime thriller! I was most interested to see what you'd say next. You said, Perhaps the woman we met in the birch copse was the identical twin of the other one ...

And perhaps Jesus was able to walk on water because the Sea of Galilee was covered in ice!

When we passed the spot again on our way down to the hotel, we walked hand in hand, and we walked fast, but at the same time we'd agreed not to panic. We both felt the same degree of fear. It was brave of you not to start running, but I had to pay the price for it, because you squeezed my knuckles so hard that my hand hurt for days afterwards. I remember the wine we had with dinner. We needed it and we drank a whole bottle and even had to ask for half a bottle more, but I also recall how I could hardly lift my glass as you'd crushed all the strength out of my hand.

I remember that night, Steinn. Now it was my turn to try to seduce you. I was very unsubtle. The thought struck me that I only had this one chance. If I didn't succeed now, we'd never manage to find each other again. I tried to tempt you with every trick I knew, and had it been just a few hours earlier, I might have made you giddy, turned you wild with desire. But nothing worked. And because you were so upset about it yourself, for like me you were certainly thinking ahead, you eventually got fairly drunk. After dinner and Calvados we'd taken a bottle of white wine up to our room, and I didn't have any. Do you remember how it all ended? With you lying down to sleep with your head at the foot of the bed next to my feet. Once I tried to stroke your chin with my toes, but you only pushed them away, not in any rough or unfriendly way, but firmly. But neither of us slept at first. We lay awake, knowing that the other was awake too, each of us feigning sleep, and finally we did sleep, you did at least, with that amount of alcohol you couldn't keep awake any longer.

I bitterly regretted that I hadn't given myself to you up there in the alder thicket before we met the Lingonberry Woman. I knew that we might well drift apart now, and I missed you already.

The longing between a couple in the same bed can sometimes be keener and more intense than a longing across continents.

The adventure was over. We conversed amicably on the boat down the fjord. We had coffee and ate west Norwegian pancakes. We disembarked from the *Nesøy* at Hella with our skis and daysacks, and the car was standing just where we'd left it, as if it felt forlorn and had been pining for us. Poor headlights and front bumper, I thought, and I believe I said it out loud. Your reply was redolent with gallows humour: She looks like us. Then we drove off.

What would we find up there on the mountain? What had we missed when we'd left the last time? Had we searched systematically for signs of blood? Or skin and hair?

But in fact that wasn't all we talked about. We had quite a pleasant drive home, considering the circumstances. Perhaps it was because we realised that this was our last car journey together. We'd begun to treat one another with a kind of post-symbiotic respect. Any spontaneous, pulse-racing detour to another love nest was out of the question now. But we behaved amicably towards each other. We were polite and considerate.

First we had to cross the fjord, then there was Lærdal, the river and the stave-church. I had a weak moment when we passed the corner by the precipice where, a week before, I'd thought you were going to kill me, or yourself. You took your right hand off the steering wheel and put your arm around me. That was comforting. Then we were up on the summits once more.

☐ And I'm travelling in the opposite direction. I'm at Gol, where I've sneaked into a wireless zone at Per's Hotel. I've read your last mail, and I'm sending from there now.

But I feel people are keeping an eye on me, because I'm not a guest here, just a passing traveller, and sometimes I think they're about to have a word with me. In the old days one used to creep into a hotel to use the toilet. Now it's just as much to use the Internet.

I just had to cross that mountain again. But I must finish now. You'll have four or five hours to yourself before I'm on the Internet again. That will be from the hotel out there, that's where I'm heading for now. I've told them to expect me, but it's coming to the end of the season, and they said I might be their only guest for the night.

☐ Are you going to Fjærland, Steinn? Then we'll be able to wave to each other in Hemsedal. We'll pass one another somewhere about there, and then there'll only be one metre and a generation separating us . . .

We saw the cold, gleaming surface of Lake Eldrevatnet, and I noticed that again your hands were shaky on the steering wheel and your foot unsteady on the accelerator. And then we arrived. You parked on the side of the road

211

and we both got out of the red Beetle; we still cared so deeply for one another, but sorrow, regret and bitterness about what had happened had severed the erotic link between us. You yelled some obscenities, you were very coarse. I didn't know you used such words. I just cried.

But the rose-pink shawl had gone. We searched for it over a large area, but even though it would have been easy to spot, we couldn't see it anywhere. Had someone found it and taken it? Or had it been blown away by the wind?

I can't remember if we felt relieved or disappointed when we found a few more shards of glass from the headlamp. So we hadn't imagined it. We had hit someone here, and at high speed. We found no other traces of the accident. There were no signs of blood, nor could we see any large stone or clod of earth that the car could have grazed.

We got back into the car and drove off. You remarked on the strange sugarloaf mound at the end of the lake, as if that had anything to do with the mystery.

All the way down Hemsedal we talked about nothing except what had happened when we'd driven up this way before. I think you were the one who began it, just as we passed the forestry road you were determined to go up when, like the incorrigible seducer you were, you'd been trying to coax me. It was unthinkable that either of us would allude to *that* escapade now.

We made an agreement. We agreed that we could discuss the fatal collision all the way home, but after we got back to Kringsjå, we would never again refer to what had occurred on that mountain road, either between ourselves or with anyone else. And that was how it was after we got back to Oslo. From then on, what happened at Lake Eldrevatnet was hardly ever spoken of as anything but *it*. These emails of mine are breaking the old agreement, but I don't believe it will conjure up any further misfortunes for us. Quite the opposite, I hope, and that's why I'm writing them.

The rose-pink shawl was no longer on the mountain – it wasn't likely to have been after that length of time, but now we had established the fact with our own eyes. Deep down I was a bit disappointed, for if we had found it again, even damaged, it would at least have been an indication that the woman we'd seen in the birch copse wasn't a person of flesh and blood, but a spirit that had shown itself to us, and then we'd have been dealing with *two* shawls, one belonging to the accident victim and one which still hung over the shoulders of the Lingonberry Woman.

Since no accident was ever reported on the news, we came to an agreement of sorts that it must have been the driver of the white van who'd taken care of the woman with the shawl, but what we just couldn't agree on was the condition she'd been in at the time. Our meeting with her near the birch copse was evidence, as far as you were concerned, that her injuries from the accident had been insignificant, while for me it was the ultimate proof of the opposite, that she'd actually died from them – and that there really *is* something there on the other side, Steinn! You thought that she'd possibly got up again straight away after the collision, and that she'd simply hitched a lift in the white van. You convinced yourself that she was going back down to Hemsedal, and that she was somehow connected to that foreign lorry. Such a solution to the mystery would have adequately explained why we hadn't heard anything on the news about a road traffic accident that night. In my view, there was no doubt that the woman with the pink shawl was either badly injured or dead when she was lifted into the van. Paradoxically, we could unite about one thing: a mere week after we'd run over the woman with the shawl, she was doing well. But you meant in this world, and I meant wherever she might be now.

We discussed the hour and time of day. If we'd only clipped her, you concluded, wasn't it a bit hasty to link her to the van that went past some minutes later? Perhaps she just walked on. Why should the van driver tell the police that he'd seen a middle-aged woman wandering across the mountain on Trunk Road 52?

'But we saw nothing of her,' I said, 'it was as if she'd

evaporated. And even if we had only grazed her, surely she should have been so annoyed with us that the first thing she'd have done when she got to civilisation was to phone the police and tell them she'd almost been knocked down and killed by a red Volkswagen with skis on its roof.'

You listened, you gripped the steering wheel more firmly than you had on the outward trip, but you shook your head and reasoned, 'She couldn't go to the police for some reason. After all, what was she doing up there in the middle of the night? You don't set off on a normal mountain hike at that time of the day, and she can hardly have gone out for a breath of fresh air either, all that way from the nearest house or hamlet. Of course you can cross the mountains at night, it doesn't get completely dark at this time of year and it's not that cold either, but in that case you do it because you have to, because you've got a particular errand, or because you're fleeing or escaping from something.'

I listened. For the sake of argument we were talking through your assumptions now.

'And *what* for example might she be running away from?' I asked.

You drove on for four or five minutes without saying anything. We'd begun to talk to each other in a completely new and strange way. We weren't lovers any more. We'd stopped chattering, we'd stopped laughing. But we were still friendly and forbearing. We wanted to help each other, but were no longer capable of doing the best for us both.

'Who or what was she running away from?' I asked again.

'From the lorry driver in the lay-by,' you said. 'Something had happened and so she simply took off up to the mountains. Perhaps she knew the locality, and it isn't that difficult to manage this pass on foot: the two valleys, west and east, are close together, almost back to back, it's only Lake Eldrevatnet that separates the two upper valleys.'

You looked at me as if pleading for help to reason further.

'For all we know that woman could have run away from a crime herself, perhaps from a brutal murder, for instance the murder of a man who'd abused her over many years, and who now was lying dead in the cab of a foreign lorry. If so, you wouldn't just run to the police.'

I was so impressed by your inventiveness that I put my hand over my mouth so you wouldn't see me laughing.

But you realised, and you replied, 'Forget that! *She* was the lorry driver herself. There was no one in the cab of that lorry when we passed it. But we saw the woman driver walking across the mountain a few minutes later. It was chilly and she'd wrapped a shawl around her shoulders. She turned away from us as if she didn't want to be recognised. That was because she'd got an appointment with the driver of a white van to meet him off the main road. They were to meet at the watershed, and something of great value would be handed over. A few kilos of white powder perhaps, or perhaps just some money, or why not powder for money? Or was something – bigger quantities of something – going to by dropped from a plane? In such cases you don't go knocking up local farmers or the police. But after being knocked down by a red Volkswagen she might have become obsessed with getting revenge, and if she was up and down the roads, it wouldn't be that surprising if, a week later, she found our Beetle at Hella. So, we'd gone to the glacier; we'd hidden up there where there was no road link, for lorries for example, and now she was coming after us. To punish us. Initially to play a trick on us. There are tricks and tricks,' you stressed. 'There are lots of ways to ruin people's lives. If you're of a resourceful bent, there are many ways of handing someone down a life sentence.'

You recently touched on something similar in one of your emails to me about a Middle Eastern wizard who'd used magic to try to make a married couple split up . . .

After all this I gave up trying to conceal that your inventiveness was getting close to comedy. I put a hand on your knee – I think you liked that, but I also think it must have been one of the very last times we displayed physical tenderness for one another – and I said, 'But the *shawl*, Steinn. If she wasn't seriously hurt, why would she have pulled off or lost her pink shawl, when the night was cold?'

I'm not sure if you believed in your own theories to any great extent. And you said as much too, that you were only trying to think rationally. There's nothing wrong with that, Steinn. But the peculiar thing about the Lingonberry Woman wasn't only that she was exactly like the woman we ran over, but that she appeared in the copse while we were touching the foxgloves – those rose-pink foxgloves, so heavy and fresh with life – and the way she disappeared again. I'd begun to develop my spiritualistic interpretation of things, and now, I mean in the car on the way home, all the way down towards Gol and Nesbyen, and on to Lake Krøderen, Sokna, Hønefoss and Sollihøgda, you at least paid attention to me, without it simply being post-symbiotic courtesy. Everything was still recent and you really *were* confused. I said nothing about the book I'd purloined from the billiard room and spent an hour reading the previous morning while you were still sleeping. But wasn't it strange too that we found that book just a few hours before our encounter with the Lingonberry Woman?

Gradually it dawned on me that our meeting with the Lingonberry Woman might be viewed as something auspicious. We, who'd always shared the same intense feeling for life, but also the same deep despair that one day it would be irrevocably over – we had suddenly been given a sign that this was only transitory, and that our souls could find an existence after this one as well. She smiled her Mona Lisa smile, mischievous and shrewd. Come! We would share in a great gift. And even today, as I write, how I would love to share that triumph with you. It needn't be too late.

But there was something else that was consoling. The woman in the rose-pink shawl was no longer in such a bad state. Didn't that make us feel a little less guilty? We'd cut short her earthly existence of course, because her body died, perhaps immediately or during the week that followed – and that remains a horrible thought – but the Lingonberry Woman revealed to us that she'd gone over to another dimension. Wasn't that why she appeared to us? To forgive us and instil us with new courage! To me she said: 'You are what I was, and I am what you will become.' Don't worry, she said. You'll become like me. You will never die ... And she had a comforting message for you as well: 'You should have got a speeding ticket, my lad.' From her point of view, I mean from her *new* point of view, you weren't guilty of anything more than a traffic offence, which any one of us might commit while we're still part of this rat race down here. What took place was no more serious than that, for our bodies are frail and ephemeral, and there is a purer and more stable existence to come.

So really she'd said much the same thing to both of us.

And then we were back at home again and weren't allowed to speak of what had happened any more. But the trauma of it remained with us, and we carried a shame and a guilt that was renewed each time we looked at one another, each time we fried an egg together, or poured one another a cup of tea or coffee.

But I've come to the conclusion that it wasn't really shame that made it impossible for us to go on living together. The pair of us could have managed to put the humiliation behind us. I think we'd have gone to the police together and turned ourselves in. Simple! We would have borne whatever punishment and disgrace we had to, each supported by the other.

Certainly you won't have forgotten what we did before putting the lid on the whole thing. Finally, and anonymously, we phoned the police. We asked them if there'd been an accident or anybody run over at the county boundary on Trunk Road 52 the night we passed through. We said we'd contacted them because we might have witnessed something. They noted the time and place, and we were told to phone back, as we'd insisted on remaining anonymous. We left it two or three days before ringing again, and the police were able to confirm that no such incident had been reported, either on the night in question or at any other time on that particularly straight and well graded section of road.

Suddenly we found that there were no traces of what had happened. This made the worldly side of things even more mysterious, and it remains a riddle to this day. There were two of us after all, and we knew we'd run a woman down. Which meant that someone other than the police and the authorities had dealt with the woman's body. Gradually too, I became convinced that we'd had contact with the woman's spirit several days after she'd passed over.

That was where the deep fissure between us lay. The conclusions I drew from what we'd experienced were quite different to yours. That was why we couldn't stay together. I immediately began to read up on spiritualist philosophy. And I'd also got the book I'd taken from the billiard room. When you saw that again, I was frightened you'd throw it at me. But then I began to read the Bible a lot too, and now I consider myself a Christian.

The risen Christ showed himself to his disciples, and I believe that that was an apparition of the same sort as the woman who revealed herself to us. We talked about this. As far as I'm concerned, the belief that Jesus first died and then his dead body came back to life again is too crude. And so I don't accept the Church's dogma on the 'resurrection of the flesh' or archaic notions about graves

---

221

opening on the Day of Judgement. I believe in the resurrection of the *soul*. In common with St Paul, I believe that after our corporeal death we'll rise again with a 'spiritual body' in quite a different dimension to the physical world we inhabit now.

I'd found a synthesis between Christianity and what to my mind was a rational belief that we have immortal souls. Although in my case it wasn't purely a matter of belief. I had *seen* an apparition of the woman we two had run over and killed, just as, according to the early Christians, Jesus' disciples had seen him after he'd 'risen from the dead'. And don't you think that Jesus too revealed himself to his disciples to show them forgiveness, in other words hope and faith?

Or in Paul's words, 'Now if this is what we proclaim, that Christ was raised from the dead, how can some of you say there is no resurrection of the dead? If there be no resurrection, then Christ was not raised; and if Christ was not raised, then our gospel is null and void, and so is your faith.'

I, who'd previously railed so bitterly against being mortal and caused us, as a kind of consolation, to get into the Beetle and head off to Jostedalsbreen glacier, I, who'd always regretted so vehemently that I'd never be able to get enough of life, had suddenly discovered a conciliatory faith in an everlasting life after this one.

———

After only two or three days our little flat was awash with books, works bought or borrowed about phenomena you called 'supernatural'. I don't think you noticed that I was also reading the Bible. But what you couldn't take was that you didn't have a faith that could match my new orientation. You saw it as a betrayal. We two had had our own sect. Now the congregation I'd left had only one adherent.

Because it wasn't the other way round. It wasn't me who couldn't manage to live with you on account of your atheism. It really wasn't. But in the long term I couldn't put up with your head-shaking rejection of my new conviction. You had no leeway. You displayed no tolerance. You showed no mercy. It was so hard to take that I had to catch that afternoon train to Bergen ...

Then a new chapter was added to this story more than three decades on. You walked out on to the balcony with a cup of coffee and suddenly found me there. It was then that, for an instant, I thought I could see myself from your perspective, and it gave me an uneasy feeling.

Let me take you on one last mental experiment. It's rather important for me because this mental experiment is also the expression of a nagging doubt that has filled me just lately. Yes, Steinn, I too can doubt.

Go back to when we were driving across the mountain that time and try to imagine there was a film camera mounted on the bonnet of the car. If it had been filming the road ahead just before the moment of collision, would you, today, be quite sure that the woman with the shawl would have come out on the film?

I'm sure you think I'm expressing myself very oddly. But I'm writing about something that's really strange.

What we called the Lingonberry Woman was a revelation from the other side. But as I've said, I'm not so sure we could have taken a photo of her, or even taped what she said. She was a spirit visiting living people. So it isn't correct to say she 'materialised'. We didn't even hear the same thing. She came to us with one thought for you and one for me. The sentences she spoke were very different, although the meaning was roughly the same.

I think I have a fairly good idea of what happened from my reading about people who've had similar experiences to ours. Let me emphasise just one important point. Spirits are of course not constrained by the time and space that exists down here in our four-dimensional, not to mention mechanical, existence. What could constrain them? So it isn't certain that the Lingonberry Woman had *already* gone over, or if it's something that lies in the future, I mean from our point of view, from our temporal corner of this mystery. She might have been an omen, and it's at least a possibility that she's still among us.

But we ran into her, you'll be thinking now, and I've

---

always argued that she either died there and then or in the following days. This is what I'm asking, Steinn. This is what has suddenly sown my small seed of doubt. It could be that what we experienced by that mountain lake was a harbinger of something that *would* come to pass, something that was going to happen.

But the smashed headlamp? And the sudden jerk of the seat belts. Yes, there was a jerk, but not a particularly big one, so we hit something, I'm not throwing any doubt on that, though whatever we hit might just as easily have been a spirit.

Even at the time I thought we hadn't suffered much damage considering the circumstances. You just drove on, after all. Would you have been able to do that if you'd collided with a reindeer or an elk?

But a little later we returned and found the shawl at least. That's true, and now, like you, I'm saying it was all a long time ago and today I'm not sure. But the police declared that there had been no accident at the spot in question.

Just to make sure that all possibilities have been covered, I'm suggesting finally that the Lingonberry Woman appeared to us on *three* occasions. First, on the path at the top of Hemsedal, then by the lake, and finally for the third time in the birch copse behind the old hotel. What do you think, Steinn?

She's never appeared to us since, not to you or me,

that was one of the first things we asked each other once we were alone again. It was very much the *two* of us she came to. Perhaps no one except the pair of us has ever seen her.

I hope this summary hasn't been too harrowing for you. Sometimes I get frightened that you may again break off contact on account of our diverging views. Perhaps you still think I'm mentally disturbed. But I know there is a place in you for a more open interpretation of the riddle we experienced out there even if, over time, we've reached very different conclusions. I remember how we talked that first day and I remember the car trip back to Oslo. It was only when I began to fill the flat with all those books that you really withdrew into yourself. And now, over thirty years later, you write that you were frightened of me.

But don't let this be the final word between us. We've been cave-dwellers together, we shouldn't forget that. And for that matter we've also been *Homo erectus*, *Homo habilis* and *Australopithecus africanus*. On a planet teeming with life, in an intensely enigmatic universe. I don't deny any of this.

The great mystery we're a part of doesn't necessarily only have a corporeal or material answer. Perhaps we're also immortal spirits, and perhaps *that* constitutes the innermost core of our individuality. All the rest of it – the stars and the dinosaurs – are just so much external detritus. Even a sun knows no more than a toad, and even a galaxy understands no more than a louse. They can only burn for their allotted span.

You've always been quick to remind me that our bodies are related to reptiles and toads. But in spite of the genetic relationship between primitive vertebrates and *Homo sapiens*, a human being is essentially different from a toad. We can stand in front of the mirror and look into our own eyes, and the eyes are the mirrors of the soul. And thus we are witnesses to our own enigma. One Indian pundit put it like this: Atheism is not believing in the glory of your own soul.

Here on earth we are both body and soul at one and the same time. But we shall survive the toad in us. The Lingonberry Woman no longer had a body of flesh and blood; she was a miracle beyond this world. I could wish that one day your eyes would be opened to the divine mystery she brought tidings of.

Then, with a pensive smile, I think back to the way we could surrender ourselves to one another, again and again, almost insatiably. And in particular I have some mental film clips from our final week out there at Fjærland. They're fine memories. And I'm not ashamed of my carnal nature, I've never even been vaguely ashamed of it, and this isn't to do with that. But today I look forward to being something much greater. More *permanent*.

Now I'm waiting for your reply.

VIII

☐ The foxgloves! You're a genius, Solrun! You may have solved an old riddle without even knowing it. But I must begin with something else.

I'm out here again. I'm sitting in the same Tower Room that we occupied. It was here I received your email a short while ago, and I've read the second part of your summary on an ultra-slim laptop sitting on the old chaise longue. It was strange. And painful. I had to walk out on to the balcony to look up at the mountains and the glacier. At something that was normal. At something that was time-less. After I'd finished reading I strolled down to the old steamship quay. It felt as if I might stumble across us there at any moment. What is time? Everything is like a film that's been double-exposed. I read it twice before deleting it just now. I've seated myself at the little table to answer.

Early this morning I left the university and cast about just as I did thirty years ago. I told you I was restless, that I'd come to a decision, and I contacted you from Gol.

I phoned Berit and told her I'd taken the car and was on my way over the mountains to spend the weekend out here and concentrate on a couple of articles I had to write. I said they concerned glaciers and the Glacier Museum. But the articles were no more than an excuse; something else was drawing me and that, of course, was your emails. I just had to come out here again. I made it in time for dinner, but after eating I rushed straight up to my room and opened your last mail, just half an hour after you sent it. I brought up the carafe of wine, and now it's standing empty on the table before me.

I came alone. I don't think you came too this time. Although, just as I passed the toll station, the idea came to me that perhaps you would pop up during the evening. I imagined us sitting in the old rotunda in the music room with coffee and liqueurs. But this is the first time I've been out here on my own. Perhaps it's something I ought to practise because I'm taken with this place, both the village itself and the old timber hotel.

It's also the first time I've driven across the mountains since we had the red Volkswagen. It felt strange, for in a way I've been driving across that mountain all my life. Day and night I've sat clutching the wheel up by the lake. Before we parked at the old ferry quay and began to dart about in space. Before we were stopped by the police in Leikanger.

When I was certain that the driver of the white van had seen our Volkswagen and had alerted the police.

We could discuss some of the niceties of your account, but I agree with most of your summary. It's accurate enough, and you bring out the nuances in our separate interpretations of what we went through and witnessed back then.

All the way from Oslo to Gol and up through Hemsedal I drove my new hybrid car and thought of you and your spiritualist view of the world. It struck me just how clearly and consistently this philosophy of yours is welded together. There isn't a trace of any scientific input, so don't misunderstand me, but it did strike me that the belief that man has an immortal soul could never quite be disproved by science. Is our consciousness simply a product of the brain's chemistry and the stimuli and environment surrounding that organ, including everything we call memory, or are we, as you so persuasively argue, more or less sovereign souls or spirits which only use the brain at this moment as a link between a spiritual dimension and the material trappings of this world? The problem is an old one and I don't think we'll ever solve it. The spiritualistic attitude to human status and ontology is perhaps too miraculous a vision for us ever to let go by the board, a discourse will always exist.

We are spirits, Steinn!
There is no death, Steinn. And there are no dead.

---

*

I'm not able to believe in anything so miraculous myself. But if things *aren't* like this, well, perhaps they should be. We are what constitute the world's consciousness. For all we know we may be the purest and most enchanted creations in the entire universe. So perhaps we don't need to excuse ourselves for going about harbouring a few optimistic dreams of a destiny beyond that of flesh and blood.

Then I note with satisfaction that despite your dualism you don't repudiate our life here on earth. Imagine if you'd said that our intimacy in the past had been due to a misunderstanding. History is replete with examples of religious fanaticism leading to a denial of everything sensual and temporal, not to mention the things that most of us consider to be the only true reality.

These thoughts ran and turned in my head all the way from Oslo. At the top of Hemsedal I pulled into that forestry track on the left of the main road, and after a few minutes' meditation I drove on.

I got up on to the mountain plateau where I've driven again and again in the feeble twilight for more than thirty years. Like some Flying Dutchman, doomed to roam the plateau, if not every day, then every night.

You remember that peculiar mound we passed just before we ran into the woman with the shawl – you mentioned the 'sugarloaf mound' yourself. It's a good description by the way, because it's a particularly striking prominence. I saw from the GPS map in the car that it has a name, and its name is, naturally enough, Eldrehaugen – the knoll of the ancient folk.

Just past the strange tumulus I found a little turning on the right-hand side of the road, where they've now put up some information boards for tourists with local and historical information. One of these stated:

Eldrehaugen is the conspicuous circular barrow just to the east of the Information Point. Eldrehaugen was the home of a band of invisible hill trolls called Åsgardsreii or Joleskreii. At midnight every Christmas Eve the Åsgardsreii or Joleskreii would come rushing out of Eldrehaugen and hurry down Hallingdal. They visited the farms and helped themselves to Christmas fare and ale. People who provided generous amounts of food and drink for them would live happy and contented. If the food was marked with a cross, the Åsgard-sreii would be offended and this could lead to misfortunes for people, property and livestock. The people of Hemsedal knew the names of several members of the band of Åsgard-sreii: Tydne Ranakam, Helge Høgføtt, Trond Høysyningen, Masne Trøst and Spenning Helle. The Åsgardsreii journeyed right down to the villages around Drammen. There they caused an uproar over the entire Christmas period, and did not return to Eldrehaugen until Twelfth Night.

———

Masne Trøst! Tydne Ranakam!

I shook my head, and when I thought of what you'd written about the person we knocked down not necessarily being an ordinary person but perhaps merely a ghost, I stood there pensively for a long time.

But the foxgloves and the 'Lingonberry Woman'! I think you might have hit the nail right on the head there.

You said that we saw the same thing. But we heard or received different messages.

We were attracted to those lush foxgloves, and you were so fascinated you had to touch them. So we must have been *thinking* exactly the same thing. Even though we didn't talk about it all the time, we were thinking almost continuously about the woman we'd hit up on the mountain. And the foxgloves were precisely the same colour as the shawl she'd been wearing across her shoulders and which we subsequently found in the heather. Not just the same colour, but exactly the same shade of rose-pink. Perhaps that was why we were so strongly drawn to them.

All at once something made us turn, as you rightly said. Maybe it was a weasel or a magpie. We turned anyway, and then we both thought that we *saw* the woman we'd run over – she was standing in the copse with the same rose-pink shawl across her shoulders.

But it was little wonder perhaps that we had approximately the same hallucination in the state of mind we were in at the time, and after, as I believe, allowing ourselves to be deluded by the fresh foxgloves and their seductive colour. Why were you attracted to them in particular? There were some attractive bluebells nearby as well.

Whether there are a hundred or a thousand or a hundred thousand different colours is an academic question. But this really was exactly the same shade. Something moved in the copse behind us, we turned and looked up, and we both thought we saw the woman with the rose-pink shawl standing there. I thought she said something, and you thought she said something else. But it's quite obvious that I'd been thinking about how I'd driven too fast across the plateau, and that you, from the age of eleven, had been plagued with ideas about the radical inescapability of having to depart this world at some point.

And you'd found that book. You'd read bits of it, so had I, and the only thing missing was the foxgloves.

Our foundations had been so shaken that we had hallucinations. We were fragile and defenceless, and so we both flipped and were completely befuddled for a few seconds.

I'm moving on tomorrow. But I'm not going to drive to Oslo across that mountain again. I'd rather go via Aurlandsdal to Hol. I've also been thinking of taking in Bergen and seeing you.

———

May I?

I could take a ferry across the fjord from Lavik to Oppedal. If the ferry times correspond, I might drive out along the fjord to Rutledal and cross over to Solund as well. I want to see the islands again. But you wouldn't be able to make that, of course. I think if you can meet me at Rutledal, or perhaps it might be even easier for you to hop on a bus to Oppedal if you can, because it's pointless to take two cars. It would be a final exploit, which you keep calling an 'escapade'. We've got a lot to talk about. I'd so like to drive you round a bit on the islands out in the mouth of the fjord. I mean all the way out to Kolgrov. We could visit Eide's Groceries on the quay and buy an ice cream – just as we did in the old days. But of course I understand if you think it's too difficult for you to get away. Give him my best regards, by the way!

For safety's sake I've reserved rooms at the Hotel Norge from tomorrow. Out here I'm now the very last guest of the season before they shut down for the winter. They've already begun to pack up and are covering the furniture with blankets and sheets.

I could arrive in Bergen tomorrow afternoon or evening. Then perhaps we could take a ride out on Sunday if you get the green light at home.

It would be strange seeing those same bays and rocks again. Now the whole island will be covered in

------

purple-flowering heather. It was at exactly this time of year we went out there before. And you're right: nearly every evening we had to go out to the point and watch the sun sink into the sea in the west.

I almost feel we belong in that kind of landscape right now.

☐ Maybe. But one day, I do believe, our souls will rise again above quite a different and more sublime horizon.

☐ But may I come to Bergen?

☐ Just come!

☐ Do you really mean that?

☐ Yes, Steinn. I only wish you were here already. Come!

☐ I hardly need conceal the fact that I've been fond of you all these years. I've thought about you every single day, and also carried on a kind of dialogue with you. So in a sense I've spent a whole lifetime with you anyway. It's strange. It's been a strange shared existence. But thank you for the past thirty years as well.

☐ I told you that I feel that I've lived like a bigamist. I've had you around me all the time as well. In addition there's been my hypersensitivity, and this told me you were thinking of me.

But Steinn ...

☐ Yes, go on. We're deleting as we go. This is just between us now.

☐ Haven't we, more than anything, been two souls that belonged together? Interlinked, I mean, like two of those inseparable photons, belonging and reacting to each other over a distance of many light years ...

I wonder if it isn't easier to feel the difference between body and soul at our age rather than when you're very young.

☐ We must talk lots more about that. We'll drive out to Solund on one of the days, won't we?

But now, after that wine, I'll go to bed. I've driven four hundred kilometres, and so perhaps I'll get to sleep straight away. Ah, sleep, what a fickle state! I can't give any guarantees about what dreams I may tangle you up in tonight. I've exhausted my genre of cosmic dreams, so perhaps they'll be very humdrum ones this time. I might try to take you for a quiet stroll round Lake Sognsvann. Anticlockwise!

Goodnight!

IX

☐ Good morning!

I've told Niels Petter that you're on your way to Bergen. At least it's done now, and that's a relief. But now I'm off out for the rest of the day. I've got such a lot to think about. We'll be seeing each other – tomorrow anyway, if not before!

☐ I'll send you an email as soon as I've got Internet access at the hotel, sometime this afternoon or evening, and we can make more detailed arrangements. Well, have a lovely day. And a good trip! Soon I'll be going down to breakfast before I check out and drive off. Yesterday evening I had the dining room entirely to myself. It was a bit lonely, but to make up for it I ordered a large carafe of wine, and perhaps that does sound rather a lot, but I had to drink your glasses as well. Eventually I was able to imagine that you were sitting across the table from me, and then I sort of began to see you alternately as you are today and as you were all those years ago. Although there isn't much difference.

...

Hi again. Well, I've arrived in Bergen after a long car journey, and am sitting in my hotel room looking out across the pond of Lille Lungegårdsvann and up towards Mount Ulriken. The lights outside are showing clearer, it's evening and, for the first time this summer, I feel the season is changing.

I witnessed a nasty road accident just south of Sognefjord, and it really shook me up, so now I'm just going to empty the minibar and glance at a newspaper before going to bed. Can we leave it that you'll ask for me in reception around 9 a.m.? Then we could perhaps drive up to Rutledal and take the ferry out to Solund?

I'm looking forward to seeing you again. And I'm looking forward to holding you too.

...

I've had breakfast and have been hanging around reception ever since. It's a quarter past nine now. Even though you haven't answered my emails, I'm assuming that you've read them and are on your way. If not, perhaps you'll give me a ring? But I'll be in my room and online the whole time.

. . .

It's midday, and I still haven't heard anything from you. I've tried to get you on your mobile, but it's been switched off all morning. I'll wait a few more hours before I phone your home number. Steinn.

☐ Steinn,

You have just put a memory stick into your computer. Solrun was wearing it round her neck when it happened, but I assure you I haven't read more than was necessary to tell me it contained an extensive correspondence between the two of you. These electronic remains belong solely to you now. I don't believe there are copies anywhere else, because she deleted them from her machine. I am now sending my final word to you on the same stick. I have also transferred the last emails you sent her in the course of that terrible day. By the time you read this, you will have found everything on this stick.

I don't know if I should say it was nice meeting you again, so for safety's sake I won't. Neither would I characterise the funeral service as worthy of Solrun. At first I wanted you to remain anonymous, and although we exchanged a few words as the mourners walked by the side of the lake, I didn't want Ingrid and Jonas, or anyone else for that matter, to know who you were. I'd hoped that you would have enough sense – enough respect, I should say – to keep away from the funeral reception at least. A funeral service is basically a public ceremony, but a funeral reception is private, it is informal and for what I would call intimate acquaintances. But you wanted to be with Solrun all the way, you said, until the very last word was spoken at the Terminus Hotel. You were adamant about that, and ultimately I had no choice but to accommodate you and introduce you to the children as an old student friend of Solrun. Call it bourgeois double standards, call it what you will, these are not the kind of situations you can practise. You're not trained to find yourself a widower all of a sudden.

At the risk of seeming petty I'd also add that right at the end of the funeral reception you were sitting and joking with Ingrid. You began to light up, as if your social instincts had just got going. Not only did you intrude into the funeral reception, but you also craved attention, you wanted an audience. And you got one. It hurt me that Ingrid laughed.

I admit that there was something between you and Solrun that she and I didn't share. I'd heard of you of course, both of you I ought to say. The two inseparables from the early 70s. When I say 'heard of' that is a gross understatement.

———

That I've sent you this memory stick and added these few lines should be viewed as an act of duty – by that I mean something I owe to her memory. It feels like handling a bequest, as these words you sent one another don't concern me. I have no idea what you both wrote about, but I did know you were corresponding. There was never anything clandestine about Solrun.

And I've been thinking. What would things have looked like today if you two hadn't met again out there at the Book Town? Would she still be alive? It is my unpleasant duty to ask this question. She is no longer able to ask herself. It can be painful having to face such a large question all alone.

When, together with uncles, aunts, nephews and nieces, we strolled from the Chapel of Hope in Møllendal to the funeral reception at the Terminus Hotel, I promised that I would get in touch one day and tell you what had happened in a bit more detail. I was also thinking about the memory stick. Didn't you realise that I was considerably embarrassed for the children's sake, indeed for the sake of the entire family? Who were you?

I'm the one who is left after her loss, I'm the one that must fill that role, and I ask for your forbearance when I say that I want no further contact with you after this.

The last time I saw her in full health was on the Saturday. I thought she had a special glow about her that morning, before we went our separate ways. She had told me you were on your way to Bergen. Was that why she was so excited? I decided not to be too possessive and suggested we might invite you home, an idea she immediately rejected. Don't even think of it, she said, as if to spare me. Well, that's what I think, or at least thought at the time. But there is something else as well.

One December day perhaps ten or fifteen years ago I gave Solrun a beautiful shawl. It was an Advent present, because as well as the shawl I'd also bought a pink begonia. I particularly remember it as the shawl and the begonia had the same rose-pink colour. I'd bought the begonia first, and then I was taken with a matching shawl in the window of Sundt's.

But she never wore the shawl. She felt uncomfortable with it from the moment she unpacked it. I asked what was wrong, and I think she said something about how she'd feel old wearing it. But then she went on to say that it reminded her of some mysterious event she'd once experienced with you. I only mention it because this was something she resurrected after we left the Book Town back in July. It was as we were driving along Lake Jølstravatnet. I made a brief comment about the weather – it had been misty all day, but now the mist was beginning to lift – and suddenly she began to chatter away about that shawl and the begonia, and then about something that had happened more than thirty years ago. But she wouldn't divulge what this 'mystical' thing was, and I merely listened to what she said without commenting. She had mentioned things before. She had talked about 'Steinn' before. She had, it's true. I suggested paying a flying visit to our summer place out at Solund, to try to blow away some of the old memories, not to mention ghosts from the past. At that she took my hand and agreed it was something that would do us good.

So that has been passed on, or should I say forwarded. It is purely for her sake that I'm doing my utmost to tie up all the loose ends of this drama.

Please understand, I don't want an answer. I'm doing no more than any spouse's duty. I'm merely tidying up after her.

On the morning we lost her, she'd taken out the old shawl again for some unknown reason. I didn't see it until we got back from the hospital, but then I found it on her desk, still carefully wrapped in the same gift box it had come in all those years before. But why? Why had she got it out again?

I placed the memory stick you're using now in that same gift box because I believe that both the shawl and the memory stick belong more to you than here with us. My clear intention is that nothing of yours should remain here in Søndre Blekeveien after this. I don't want Jonas prying into what you and Solrun wrote to each other, and I have no wish that Ingrid should inherit this shawl. And then, for my own sake, I have to try to move on. There are many things to take care of after a death – accounts to close, subscriptions to cancel and just general winding up. And you were on the list.

I had planned to go to my office that morning, and she'd said she was going to visit a woman friend. She made it clear for once that she wouldn't be home for dinner, and she hinted that she would be late. 'Very late,' she said.

She didn't say who this woman friend was or where she lived, and so it's still a mystery to me why she travelled north to Sogn that morning. She'd never mentioned a friend there, but she did stipulate that she would be away all day.

Did she intend going all the way out to Solund, where we've holidayed quite a bit these past few years? But if she did, why didn't she say so, why didn't she take the car and why did she start walking along that busy motorway?

Because it was on the E39 just south of Oppedal, or more accurately where the road to Brekke and Rutledal branches off, that she was knocked down. The bus driver confirmed that she'd got on in Bergen, and he also remembered that she'd left the bus at Instefjord, which is a virtual dead end as regards transport, and that when the same bus did the return run from Oppedal she was still there waiting.

Solrun could be unpredictable. But that doesn't matter any more. I assume it wasn't you arriving from the north on your way from Oslo to Bergen. Didn't you come by train?

She was run over by an articulated lorry a few kilometres south of Sognefjord. The speed limit is eighty kilometres an hour, but the lorry was doing almost double that down the long descent towards Instefjord. The visibility was poor, and the driver, a young man who was trying to catch a ferry from Oppedal, is facing a court case and, hopefully, a long prison sentence.

Even *he* turned up for the funeral service. But at least he had the sense to keep away from the funeral reception. Otherwise I would have thrown him out. I would have phoned the police.

I was doing a little extra work at my office that Saturday when they rang from the hospital. They told me what had happened; they said she had been picked up by air ambulance and said she was critical. I rushed out and phoned Ingrid and Jonas from the taxi. I had a few minutes with her before the children arrived. She was in a bad way, but then she opened her eyes, and with a look full of crystal clarity she said, 'What if I was wrong? Perhaps it was Steinn who was right!'

It isn't only from children and drunks that you hear the truth. The dying too can let fall words of wisdom.

Perhaps you were *right*, Steinn. Doesn't that sound good?

It's out of a sense of duty towards Solrun that I pass on her very last greeting. Or should I say remark? I have no idea what she was referring to. But perhaps you have. I must admit though to an uneasy feeling, a suspicion.

All in all, I can't help thinking that it was a very fateful reunion you had out there at that hotel. She was never herself again.

I know, and perhaps you do too, that she was a very religious person. Through thick and thin she had an unshakeable faith in a life after this one. Could I hazard a guess that you are more of a rationalist? If nothing else, as a climatologist you're a scientist. I would venture that you and Solrun were poles apart when it came to life philosophies.

But even so I have been asking myself if we wouldn't have done better to leave Solrun's notions alone. She was a beacon, she was a blaze, and she had something almost clairvoyant about her.

Perhaps it was Steinn who was right?

She stared up at me with panic in her eyes. And there I saw an inconsolable sorrow, an intense agitation and an unbearable desperation. But then she was gone again, until she rallied one last time. Then she just looked up at me, empty and helpless. There was nothing more to say. Maybe she still had the strength to say goodbye, but she didn't.

She had lost her faith, Steinn. She was completely void. She was so desolate and empty.

What did she mean when she said you were the one who was right? Is that really so important? To be *right*? Or even to have the will or ability to sow the nagging seeds of doubt in another person's faith? No, as I've said, I don't want an answer. It's over.

I don't quite know why, but it struck me that you entered Solrun's life and mine like some peevish, old-fashioned character of Ibsen's. A man from the sea almost. Or as some truth-addicted Gregers Werle? In that case I'll willingly take on another role from *The Wild Duck* – Relling, the respecter of self-delusion. I'll sit in her golden attic room and gaze out across the city.

Solrun said something one day recently about how she might go out to Solund and say goodbye to the sea for the winter. It wasn't like her to plan such jaunts on her own. Perhaps the pair of you were to take leave of the sea? The pair who made off so quickly into the mountains that day in July.

I don't really know why I'm asking, because I want no response, and it hasn't any conceivable importance any more.

You came to Bergen all right! But you came too late. Then you phoned here on Sunday afternoon when everything was over. We had just got back from the hospital. It was Ingrid who answered the phone, but she only said she didn't know who you were, and that she couldn't talk to you. I was sitting hunched over the dining table and told Ingrid that I knew about you but couldn't face talking to you either. Jonas was

---

the one who eventually picked up the phone and told you what had happened. I let him do it.

And what did you do then? Remain in Bergen until the funeral? Or did you go out and stare at the sea?

These questions are rhetorical.

From now on I would like all contact to cease, and hope you will respect this wish. For a long time to come the children and I will have more than enough to do looking after one another.

She's left an emptiness behind her up here at Skansen. There were people who cared about Solrun on our side of the mountains too.

That's everything.

Niels Petter